SV

'Down on your knees, my child,' said Father Dirrag, 'reveal that part of your body which raises the fury of our Lord. Forget yourself and let it happen!'

Miss Eradice obeyed immediately. Holding a book in her hands, she knelt down in front of a little prayer stool. Then she lifted her skirts about her waist, revealing her snow-white, perfectly rounded buttocks which tapered downward into her two gorgeous firm-fleshed thighs.

'Lift your skirts just a little higher, dear daughter,' urged the good priest, 'there is no need for you to hide your beauty from the sight of the Lord . . .'

Sweet Sins

Therese & Angelica

Anonymous

HEADLINE

ISBN 0 7472 3498 1

Typeset by Medcalf Type Ltd, Bicester

Printed and bound in Great Britain by
Collins, Glasgow

HEADLINE BOOK PUBLISHING PLC
Headline House
79 Great Titchfield Street
London W1P 7FN

Therese

Are you serious, my dear count? Do you really want me to write down my story? Do you truly desire that I recount the mystical happenings between Miss Eradice and the Most Reverend Father Dirrag? That I tell you all about the affair between Madame Catherine and the abbot? And you request from a girl who has never written anything in all her life that she give a detailed description of everything that took place. Milord, you are insisting upon a lascivious painting which shows everything I have told you about; and of which we, ourselves, have been a part. And at the same time you want me to recount the metaphysical contemplations, telling you about the tremendous impact they made upon me. Truly, my dear count, this is a task way too heavy for my feeble powers. Besides, Eradice was my best friend, Father Dirrag was my confessor, and I have nothing but gratitude for dear Madame Catherine and the abbot. Am I to betray the trust of those people toward whom I feel the greatest admiration? Because the deeds of the one and the good advice of the others have slowly opened my eyes against the prejudice of youth. But then, you say, if their advice and example have made you happy, why shouldn't you make others happy and contribute to their pursuits with the wisdom you have learned? What is that fear which prevents you from writing down the truth which can be of such tremendous value to the society of man?

All right, my dear benefactor, I shall no longer resist your reasoning. I will write everything down. Well-read people will have to excuse my lack of style which may occur from time to time for the sake of clarity, and I don't

2

give a hoot about those self-styled fault-finders. No, your sweet and loving Therese will never deny you any of your wishes. I will show you every little fold of her tender heart, from early childhood, and you will get to know every nook and cranny of her trusting soul. I will give you an exact description of every little adventure which has slowly but surely carried her, so to speak, without her doing anything for it, step by step to the highest peaks of lasciviousness and delight.

Foolish people! You, who believe you have it within your power to kill the passions which Nature has given you! No, they are God's work! And you want to destroy those passions, guide them into narrow paths. Idiots! You pretend to be new creators, more powerful and wise than the Old One? Will you never realize that He saw that everything was good, and that everything is exactly as it was meant to be? That everything belongs to God and not to you? That it is as difficult to create a thought as it is to make an arm, or an eye, or a leg?

My career is undeniable proof of these eternal truths. Since early childhood I had been told that I should harbor love for virtue and disgust for vice. I had been told: 'You will only find happiness in proportion to living these Christian and moral virtues. All that causes you to serve from that path is vile and unnatural, it is vice! And vice causes depravity and wickedness and their natural results are shame and guilt!' Convinced of the excellence of these teachings, I have severely tried to live up to them till I had reached the age of twenty-five years. I will show you how far I have been successful.

I was born in the province of Vencerop. My father was a good, solid citizen, a merchant, in a nice little town where everyone was happy and the atmosphere free of troubles. The amorous life seemed to be the only thing in which the people were interested. They began to love as soon as they started to think, and their only reason for thinking was to dream up different ways and means to increase the pleasures of making love. In my mother the vivaciousness of the women from her homeland was admirably blended with the sensibility of those in her new country. My parents lived modestly from their small income and from the money which was brought in by father's business ventures. Their labors neither increased nor diminished their income noticeably because father paid a young widow who had a shop down the street. Mother, however, had her own income from a rich nobleman who was kind enough to honor my father with his friendship. Everything was marvellously well-organized and both parties knew exactly where they stood. Never had any marriage created a better impression of unity than theirs.

The years passed in laudable harmony, and then, after ten years, my mother became pregnant and brought me into the world. My birth caused her to suffer enormously and brought her a fate worse than death. Due to a sudden movement during the birth pangs, a big tear developed. This made her swear off forever the joys which had been responsible for my birth.

The changes in my parental home were enormous. My mother became pious. The frequent visits of the ardent marquess ceased, because my mother had told him to stop seeing her. In his place she received Father Guardian, a Capuchine monk. My mother's need for loving tenderness changed. Out of necessity she started giving to God what she had been giving to the marquess out of inclination and temperament.

Father died when I was still a babe in the cradle. For

some reason, unknown to me, mother moved to the famous harbor town of Volno. The most amorous woman had turned into the most chaste, and possibly also the most virtuous creature that had ever lived.

I was barely seven years old when my sweet and dear mother, who was constantly worried about my health and well-being, noticed that I rapidly lost weight. A famous doctor was called into consultation about my mysterious illness. I was ravenously hungry all the time, yet I had no fever and felt no pain. Nevertheless, I lost my vivaciousness and my poor legs were barely capable of carrying my skinny frame. Mother feared for my life; she never left me out of her sight and she made me sleep with her in the big bed. Who can describe her enormous surprise when, one night, she discovered that I was rubbing in my sleep that part of my body which makes me differ from a boy? It seemed to her that the rhythmic rubbing gave me joys which one would expect in a fifteen-year-old girl but which are generally not expected from a little one.

Mother scolded me thoroughly. She asked me who had taught me the horrors she had just witnessed. I started to cry and answered her that I did not know what I had done to upset her so much, and that I had no idea what she meant with all those expressions that rolled from her lips. All those words — fingering, coming, indecency and mortal sin — meant absolutely nothing to me. The naiveté of my answers convinced mother of my innocence. I fell asleep. The tickling started again. And . . . mother scolded me again. After she had observed me closely for several nights there was no longer any doubt in her mind. The strength of my passions caused me to do in my sleep what so many poor nuns do in their waking and praying hours. Mother decided to tie my hands close together behind my back so that it would become impossible for me to continue my nightly exercises.

Soon I had regained my health and former strength. I discontinued the vile habit but, unfortunately, my secret passion grew. When I was about nine or ten I noticed a curious unrest and I felt desires well up in me whose goal I did not know. I often played with other little girls and boys of my age in the attic or some quiet little room. We had our little games: one of us was elected to be the teacher; the smallest offence was punished with the rod. The boys lowered their little pants and the girls lifted their skirts and petticoats. We viewed each other with great curiosity. Five or six little behinds were the object of intense concentration; we admired them, petted them and whipped them. The wee-wees of the boys — that's what we called them — were little playthings for the girls. We took them between our fingers and made little dolls out of those instruments, having no idea of their use and value. Then our little behinds got their turn. They were kissed and caressed, too. Only our centers of joy were completely ignored. Nobody bothered about them. Why this terrible neglect? I don't know. But, those were our games; simple Nature guided them, and I tell things as they actually happened.

After I had abandoned myself for about two years to these harmless escapades, mother placed me in a convent. I must have been about eleven years old. The main interest of the old nun was to prepare me for my first confession. I was without fear for this first judgment, because I had no qualms whatsoever. I told old Father Guardian, the Capuchine monk who also advised my mother's conscience, all the stupid little sins a girl of my age was supposed to commit. After I had told him every single little mistake I believed I had made, the good father said to me, 'One of these days you will become a saint, if you follow all the good advice your dear mother has given you. Especially, let me warn you, never, never listen to the devil of the flesh. I am your mother's confessor, and she has told me of your lack of chastity, this foulest of all evils. I have been seriously concerned about you. But, I am happy to discover that she has made a mistake. The illness from which you suffered four years ago must have given her that idea. Without her infinite care, my dearest child, you would have been doomed; body and soul. Yes, I am sure that those certain movements she noticed must have been involuntary and I am convinced that the conclusion she drew in regard to your salvation was absolutely wrong.'

The strange language of my father confessor upset me terribly and I asked him what on earth I had done to give my mother such horrible ideas about the state of my immortal soul. He told me without further ado exactly what had happened, in clear, plain language. He also said that the immediate steps my mother had taken to correct my terrible mistake could have saved me from the most horrible consequences. He also added that he hoped I would never have to find out those evils on my own person.

His words reminded me suddenly about those games in the attic about which I have told you. My cheeks were covered with a deep red blush and my eyes dropped to the floor. I remained mute and silent. For the first time I had an inkling that our harmless little games could have been sinful. The priest asked me why I suddenly became so quiet and sad. I told him everything. Then he wanted to know more and started to press for details. The innocence of my expressions, my unembarrassed description of our positions and the simple, yet open statements about our pleasures, convinced him even more of my innocence. He repproached me about those games but he did it wisely and carefully and with a tact which is highly unusual for a servant of the church. But the expressions he used proved without a doubt that he had guessed my temperament correctly. He ordered me to fast, pray and think. To this arsenal he added yet another weapon. I had to wear a penitent's hair shirt. This, he said, would aid me in the fight against my passions.

'Never,' he told me, 'never ever touch with your hand that filthy part of your body. Don't even cast a glance upon it. It is the very apple which tempted Adam and which caused the fall of the race of Man and the expulsion from Paradise. In it lives the devil who brought us to our doom. It is his home, his throne. Don't allow yourself to be captured by this enemy of God and Man. Soon, Nature will cover this filthy part of your belly with ugly hairs, like those of the wild beasts in the forest. It is our punishment to remind you that you have to be ashamed of it, and from then on it will be hidden in darkness, and, God grant you, forgetfulness. But, my child, be even more careful with that piece of flesh the little boys have. You may have thought it fun up there in the attic, but, my daughter, that piece of flesh is the snake who tempted the Mother of all of us. Eve. Don't allow yourself to become dishonoured by touching this piece of meat, or even by looking upon it. It is intent upon biting you, poisoning you, and, if it can, gorging itself upon you.'

'But how, Reverend Father,' I answered, extremely excited, 'is that possible? Could it really be a snake, and is it truly as dangerous as you say it is? I thought that it was a rather soft and harmless little animal. And it never bit me or any of my girl friends. I tell you it has a very tiny mouth and absolutely no teeth at all. I have looked it over very carefully . . .'

'Go, my dearest child,' interrupted my father confessor. 'Believe me when I tell you that the snakes you have held so boldly in your innocent little fingers were too young and too small to cause all the dangers which I just described to you. But, I assure you, they will grow; they will become heavier, longer, and firmer. They will throw themselves upon you, pump their unholy venom into you. You will have to learn right now to fear the results of their ruthless onslaught. They are scheming and plotting monstrosities, eager to squirt their poison, intent upon destroying your body and your eternal soul.'

After this and several other lessons, the good father let me go, leaving me in a state of terrible confusion and inner turmoil.

I returned to my room and stayed there for several days, fasting and praying. The words he had spoken to me had made a great impression upon my young imagination, but nevertheless, the thoughts about those pretty little snakes did not leave me. They seemed more charming than ever, despite the terrible sermon which the well-meaning priest had given about them. The desire to touch and hold one was stronger than the fear to leave them alone. Nevertheless, I kept my promise. I resisted the temptations of my vile temperament. I prayed, I fasted and did penitence, and soon I had become a veritable example of virtue.

Oh, the struggles I have fought, my dear count! Finally my mother took me out of that damned convent! I had barely turned sixteen when my feverish thoughts had weakened my body. It was obvious that two different passions ruled my body and soul. I was unable to make the one reach accord with the other. On the one hand

I felt a true love for God: I wanted to serve Him with all my heart in the exact way they had told me. He wished to be served. On the other hand I noticed fierce desires without being able to guess their purpose. The picture of the pretty snake had burned itself indelibly into my soul. It was perennially before my mind's eye, in my waking as well as in my sleep hours. Sometimes I became so excited that I believed to hold the snake in my hands; I caressed its head, I admired its noble, proud posture, its firm erectness, even though I had no idea of the purpose of this beautiful animal. My heart would pound with unusual speed; at the peak of my excitement, or in the middle of my dreams, a voluptuous quiver would run through my body. It nearly drove me out of my mind. The apple attracted my hand as if it were a powerful magnet, my finger would take the place of the snake.

Excited by the many possibilities of delight, I was incapable of any other thoughts, and even if the earth had opened up before me and the tortures of hell had yawned at me, I would have been incapable of stopping. Oh, the useless pangs of conscience! I would wallow in lasciviousness. But the restlessness afterward! Fasting, flagellation, prayer and penitence were my only recourse. I practically drowned in my own tears of remorse. Gradually these practices destroyed my passions. But, they not only wrecked my sensuality, they ruined my health as well. I had ultimately reached a state of weakness which had carried me to the brink of the grave. Finally my mother decided to take me away from the convent . . .

Answer me, treacherous or ignorant priests, who credit us with nonexistent crimes: Who has implanted both passions in my soul? Those two desires which I have been unable to reconcile: My love for God, and my desire for carnal knowledge? Was it Nature or the devil? Make up your minds! Or do you really dare to insist that either the devil or Nature are more powerful than God who created both of them? Because if they are less powerful than God, then it must be Him, Who has given me both passions; then it must have been His handiwork.

But, you will undoubtedly answer me, God has given you the intelligence to make up your own mind.

Indeed. But not to decide about my will. My intelligence has made it possible to discern the two different passions which struggled for the possession of my body and mind. Through them I have been made to understand that both are gifts of God, just like everything else is a gift of God. But even though my intelligence had made this clear to me, I still did not have the willpower.

But God has given you the power over your own free will, you will say. You are free to decide the path of good or the path of evil.

That is the purest form of nonsense, a mere play of words. The strength of this will, and the momentary freedom to decide, are directly proportional to the strength of the passions and desires that drive us along the path of life. For instance, I am theoretically free to kill myself, to throw myself out of the window. Not at all true! As long as my love for life is stronger than the desire to kill myself, I'll never commit suicide.

But, you will say, you are absolutely free to give alms to the poor, or to hand a hundred gold francs to your father confessor, if you happen to have that amount in your pocket.

That, too, is not true. If the desire to keep your money is stronger than to throw it away on a useless forgiveness of imaginary sins, then it is rather obvious to me that one does not wish to throw his money away. In one word, everyone can, with a simple test, convince himself that intelligence is only a means to show how strong a certain desire really is and whether giving in to that particular desire will cause pleasure or remorse. And the result of this intelligent realization is our so-called free will. But this will depends as much upon our passions and desires as the movement of a scale which will sink toward the level of a four-pound weight if we counterbalance it with only three pounds on the other end.

But, you will ask, is it then not my own free will to order a bottle of Burgundy or a bottle of champagne with my meal? Am I not master of my own destiny and choose to stroll in the Tuileries or sit at a sidewalk café on a boulevard?

I admit that in all cases where the decision is rather irrelevant, where our desires and wishes keep each other more or less in balance, our lack of freedom is not immediately apparent. From a distance we don't notice the single objects any longer. But as soon as we come close to those objects we notice very clearly that our lives are influenced heavily by the mechanical laws of checks and balances. We realize that Nature operates consistently by this one law. Set yourself down to dinner. You are served oysters. Obviously you will select champagne.

But, you will answer, I could have selected Burgundy. I was perfectly free to do so.

I say: No! Obviously, some other reason, a different desire which would have been stronger than the first, natural impulse, could have caused you to drink Burgundy. But in that case it would have been this strong, and rather odd desire which would have influenced your so-called free will.

Let's assume you are strolling in the Tuileries and at the terrace of the Feuillants you see a charming woman of your acquaintance, and you decide to walk over and talk to her. Meanwhile, for some other reason, you suddenly decide to continue your stroll, or follow some other pleasure or business, and you are not going to talk to her. Whatever you decide to do, it is always some desire which is stronger than the other that causes your ultimate decision, quite independent from your will.

To admit that Man is a free agent, one must assume that his decisions are entirely free from outside influences. And as soon as his decisions are caused by two or more struggling inner desires, implanted in him by Nature, he is no longer free. The strength of one desire or the other will influence his actions as surely as a four-pound weight on a scale causes the three-pound weight to rise.

And I also ask you: What prevents you thinking about these questions the same way I do, and why can't I bring myself to have the same opinion as you? Undoubtedly your answer will be that your thoughts, your opinions and your feelings force you to believe the way you do. This consideration must convince you therefore that it is not agreeable to you to think as I do, and consequently that it does not depend upon me to think as you do. And out of all this it follows clear as crystal that we cannot believe as we please. And since we seemingly are not free to think as we please, how on earth can we act with total freedom? Our thinking is the case and our actions are merely the result of our thinking. And is it possible that out of a cause which is not free, a free action can result? Such reasoning would hold an absolute contradiction.

I will show you the truth of this reasoning with the following true story. Gregory, Damon and Phillip are three brothers. They have been educated by the same teachers till they are twenty-five years old. They have never been separated from one another, they have received exactly the same upbringing, and they have had precisely the same lessons in morals and religion. Nevertheless, Gregory loves to drink wine, Damon loves to wench, and Phillip is extremely devout. What was the cause of this triple diversity in the will of these three brothers? It cannot be their knowledge of what is good and evil, because the same teachers have given them the same lessons. Each one of them must have had different principles and different passions carried within him since birth, and despite the similarity in upbringing and education they must have had a different will.

I'll go one step further. Gregory, who loves the wine, is an honorable man, a charming host and the best friend a person might wish to have, as long as he is sober. The moment he has tasted the magic drink he changes and becomes vicious, lazy and quarrelsome. He would cut the throat of his best friend with pleasure. Was Gregory master over the changes that came over him? No, not in the least, because when he was sober he abhorred the things he did when he was drunk from the wine. Of course, a lot of stupid idiots admired the abstinence of Gregory who did not like women, the sobriety of Damon who could not stand wine, and the piousness of Phillip who hated both wine and women, but who got the same pleasure out of his devotions which the others derived from either their wine or their wenches. That is how most people lie to themselves with their provincial ideas about human vices and virtues.

I would draw the following conclusions: The organs of the body, the nervous system, the presence of certain juices; their presence and their strength or weakness influence our will during important decisions we have to make in our lifetime. Therefore, there are passionate people, wise people, and crazy people. The crazy ones are neither more nor less free than all the others, because they are what they are according to the same principles. Nature never varies. So, if we assume that Man is free to act as he wants and can plot his own path through life, we make him equal to God . . .

But, let's go back to my story!

As I said, I was almost dead when my mother decided to take me out of the convent. My entire body was exhausted; with my yellowish skin and my thin lips I looked like a living skeleton. My piousness had turned me into a suicidal maniac and I surely would have died if I had not returned in time to my mother's home. The very good doctor whom she had sent to me in the convent had immediately recognized the source of my illness. that divine juice which is capable of giving us physical delight, the only delight whose enjoyment does not leave one filled with bitterness, that juice whose outflow is just as necessary as the intake of good food, that juice had left the vessels for which it was intended and had penetrated other vessels in my body. That was the reason that my entire body was sick. My mother was advised to look posthaste for a husband for me; this was the only way to save my life. Mother talked very kindly to me about the prospect, but I was so caught up in my own prejudices that I harshly told her I would rather die than displease God by contracting a marriage which would be a despicable affair at best and which He only tolerated in His infinite goodness. All the reasons she gave me were of no interest to me; my weakened constitution left me without any desire for this world and the only happiness I counted on was that of the next world which I had heard so much about from the nuns.

I continued my pious exercises with undiminished fervour. I had been told about the famous Father Dirrag;

15

I looked him up and he became the advisor of my soul. His most fervent visitor, Miss Eradice, soon became my best friend.

You know, my dear count, the history of these two famous people. I have no intention of repeating everything that has been said about those two. But I have been witness to a rather strange occurrence and maybe you would enjoy listening to my side of this story — if only to convince you that, even though Eradice ultimately knew what she was doing, she allowed the old lecher to embrace her because she was betrayed by her own voluptuous piousness.

Miss Eradice had become my dearest girl friend; she confided her deepest secrets to me. We did the same religious exercises, we thought about the same godly things and we were in complete agreement about the salvation of our eternal souls. Possibly we also had the same temperament. Anyway, we were inseparable. We were both extremely virtuous and our one overriding passion was the desire to be considered very pious. Secretly we hoped to achieve the sanctity which would enable us to perform miracles. This passion ruled my friend so powerfully that she would gladly have borne all the tortures of the early Christian martyrs if she had been told that it would enable her to raise a second Lazarus from the dead. And, Father Dirrag had developed his gift to perfection to make her believe whatever he wanted.

Rather vainly, Eradice had told me on several occasions that Father Dirrag had assured her in secrecy that she only needed a few more steps to achieve complete sanctity. She had, so she told me, visited him frequently in his home, where he had held various confidential sessions with her. God had told him in a dream that she would soon be capable of performing great miracles if she would allow him, Father Dirrag, to help her practice virtue and mortification of the flesh.

Jealousy and envy are two normal human vices, but pious virgins are most prone to them.

Eradice must have noticed that I was envious, begrudged her her happiness and, worst of all, did not seem to believe her! I must admit that I was very surprised about her tales of his confidential talks with her at his home, especially since the good father had always carefully avoided talking to me, one of his most ardent penitents, about anything else but mortification of the flesh. And I knew another penitent, also a good friend of mine, who, like Eradice, also carried the stigmata of our Lord. He had never been as confidential to her as he had been to Eradice, and this girlfriend, too, had all the attributes of a saint. No doubt, my sad face, my yellowish complexion, my utter lack of any sign of stigmata were enough reasons for the venerable Father Dirrag not to have any confidential talks with me at his home. The possibility existed that he saw no reason to take on the extra burden of spiritual works on my behalf. But to me it was a bone of contention. I became very sad and I pretended not to believe any of Eradice's stories.

This irritated Eradice no end. She offered to let me become an eyewitness to her happiness that next morning. 'you will see for yourself,' she contended heatedly, 'how strong my spiritual exercises are, how the good father guides me from one degree of mortification to the next with the purpose of making a saint out of me. You will be a witness to the delight and ecstasy which are a direct result of these exercises and you will never again doubt how marvellous these exercises are. Oh, how I wish, my dearest Therese, that my example would work its first miracle upon you. That you might be spiritually strengthened to totally deny the flesh and follow the only path which will lead you to God!'

We agreed that I would visit her the next morning at five o'clock. I found her in prayer, a book in her hand. She said to me, 'The holy man will arrive soon, and God shall be with him. Hide yourself in that little alcove, and from there you can see and hear for yourself the miracles of Divine Love wrought upon me by the venerable father confessor. Even to such a lowly creature as I.'

Somebody knocked quietly on the door. I fled into the alcove; Eradice turned the key and put it in her skirt pocket. There was, fortunately, a hole in the alcove door, covered with a piece of tapestry. This made it possible for me to see the entire room, without, however, running the risk of being seen myself.

The good father entered the room and said to Eradice, 'Good morning, my dearest sister in the Lord, may the Holy Spirit of Saint Francis protect you forever.'

She wanted to throw herself at his feet, but he lifted her off the floor and ordered her to sit down next to him upon the sofa. Then the holy man said, 'I cannot repeat too often the principles which are going to become the guidelines for your future way of life, my dear child. But, before I start my instructions, tell me, dear child, are the stigmata, those miraculous signs of God's everlasting favour, still with you? Have they changed at all? Show them to me.'

Eradice immediately bared her left breast, under which she bore the stigma.

'Oh, oh, please, dear sister! Cover your bosom with this handkerchief! (He handed her one.) These things were not created for a member of our society; it is enough for me to view the wound with which the holy Saint

Francis has made you, with God's infinite mercy. His favourite. Ah! it is still there. Thank the Lord, I am satisfied. Saint Francis still loves you; the wound is rosy and clean. This time I have with me a part of our dear Saint's sacred rope; we shall need it for our mortification exercises. I have told you already, my dear sister, that I love you above all my other penitents, your girl friends, because God has so clearly marked you as one of the beloved sheep in His flock. You stand out like the sun and the moon among the other planets and stars. Therefore I have not spared any trouble to instruct you in the deepest secrets of our Holy Mother Church. I have repeatedly told you, dearest sister, 'Forget yourself, and let it happen.' God desires from Mankind only spirit and heart. Only if you can succeed in forgetting the existence of your body will you be able to experience Him and achieve sainthood. And only as a saint will you ever be able to work miracles.

'My little angel, I cannot help scolding you, since I noticed during our last exercises that your spirit is still enslaved by your body. How can that be? Couldn't you at least be a little bit like our saintly martyrs? They were pinched with red-hot irons, their nails were torn off their feet and fingers, they were roasted over slow fires and yet . . . they did not experience pain. And why not? Because their mind was filled with pure thoughts of God's infinite glory! The most minute particle of their spirit and mind was occupied with thoughts of His immense glory. Our senses, my dear daughter, are mere tools. But, they are tools that do not lie. Only through them can we feel, only through them can we understand the evil and the good. They influence our bodies as well as our souls. They influence our bodies as well as our souls. They enable us to perceive what is morally right and what is morally wrong.

'As soon as we touch something, or feel, or hear, minute particles of our spirit flow through the tiny holes in our nerves. They report the sensations back to our soul. However, when they are filled completely with the love they owe their God and Creator, when YOU are so full of love and devotion that none of these minute particles can do anything else but concentrate on the Divine Providence, when the entire spirit is given to the contemplation of our Lord, then and only then is it impossible for any particle to tell our spirit that the body is being punished. You will no longer feel it.

'Look at the hunter. His entire being is filled with only one thought: his prey! He does not feel the thorns that rip at him when he stalks through the forest, nor does he notice cold or heat. True, these elements are considerably weaker than the mighty hunter, but . . . the object of his thoughts! Ah, that is a thousand times stronger than all his other feelings put together. Would you feel the feeble blows of the whip when your soul is full of the thoughts of happiness that is about to be yours! You must be able to pass this all-important test. We must know for sure, if we want to be able to work miracles, whether we can reach this degree of perfection, whether we can wholly immerse ourselves in God!

'And we shall win, dear daughter. Do your duty, and be assured that thanks to the rope of the holy Saint Francis, and thanks to your pious contemplations, this holy exercise will end for you with a shower of unspeakable delight. Down on your knees, my child! Reveal that part of your body which raises the fury of our Lord; the pain you will feel shall bring your soul in close contact with God. I must repeat again: 'Forget yourself, and let it happen!'

Miss Eradice obeyed immediately without uttering a

20

single word. Holding a book in her hands, she knelt down in front of a little prayer stool. Then she lifted her skirts about the waist, showing her snow-white, perfectly rounded buttocks that tapered into two gorgeous alabaster, firm-fleshed thighs.

'Lift your skirts a little higher, my dear child,' he said to her, 'it does not look proper yet. Good, good . . . that's a lot better. Put the prayer book down, fold your hands and lift up your soul to God. Fill your mind with thoughts about the eternal happiness which has been promised you!'

The priest pulled up his footstool and kneeled next to her, bending slightly backward. He lifted his cowl and tied it to the rope around his waist. Then he took a large birch rod and held it in front of my penitent friend who kissed it devoutly.

Piously shuddering I followed the whole procedure with full attention. I felt a sort of horror which is very difficult to describe. Eradice did not say a word. The priest gazed upon her thighs with a fixed stare, his eyes sparkling. He did not let his gaze wander for a single moment. And I heard him whisper softly, full of admiration, 'Oh, God, what a marvellous bosom. My Lord, those gorgeous tits!'

Now he bent over and then he straightened up again, murmuring biblical language. Nothing escaped his vile curiosity. After a few minutes he asked the penitent if her soul was prepared.

'Oh yes, venerable Father! I can feel my soul separate itself from my unworthy flesh. I pray you, begin your holy work!'

'It is enough. Your soul will be happy!'

He said a few prayers and the ceremony started with three fairly light blows of the rod, straight across her firm buttocks. This was followed by a recitation from The Bible. Thereupon another three blows, slightly stronger than the first ones.

After he had recited five or six verses, and interrupted each of them the same way as before, I suddenly noticed to my utter surprise that the venerable Father Dirrag had opened his trousers. A throbbing arrow shot out of his clothing which looked exactly like that fateful snake which my former father confessor had so vehemently warned me about.

The monster was as long and as thick and as heavy as the one about which the Capuchine monk had made all those dire predictions about. I shuddered with delightful horror. The red head of this snake seemed to threaten Eradice's behind which had taken on a deep pink colouration because of the blows it had received during the Bible recitation. The face of Father Dirrag perspired and was flushed a deep red.

'And now,' he said, 'you have to transport yourself into total meditation. You must separate your soul from the senses. And if my dear daughter has not disappointed my pious hopes, she shall neither feel, nor hear, nor see anything.'

And at that very moment this horrible man loosed a hail of blows, letting them whistle down upon Eradice's naked buttocks. However, she did not say a word; it seemed as if she were totally insensitive to this horrendous whipping. I noticed only an occasional twitching of her bottom, a sort of spasming and relaxing at the rhythm of the priest's blows.

'I am very satisfied with you,' he told her, after he had punished her for about five minutes in this manner. 'The time has come when you are going to reap the fruits of your holy labours. Don't question me, my dear daughter, but be guided by God's will which is working through me. Throw yourself, face down, upon the floor; I will now expel the last traces of impurity with a sacred relic. It is a part of the venerable rope which girded the waist of the holy Saint Francis himself.'

The good priest put Eradice in a position which was rather uncomfortable for her, but extremely fitting for what he had in mind. I had never seen my girl friend in such a beautiful position. Her buttocks were half-opened and the double path to satisfaction was wide open.

After the old lecher had admired her for a while, he moistened his so-called rope of Saint Francis with spittle, murmured some of the priestly mumbo-jumbo which these gentlemen generally use to exorcize the devil, and proceeded to shove the rope into my friend.

I could watch the entire operation from my little hideout. The windows of the room were opposite the door of the alcove in which Eradice had locked me up. She was kneeling on the floor, her arms were crossed over the foot-stool and her head rested upon her folded arms. Her skirts, which had been carefully folded almost up to her shoulders, revealed her marvellous buttocks and the beautiful curve of her back. This exciting view did not escape the attention of the venerable Father Dirrag. His gaze feasted upon the view for quite some time. He had clamped the legs of his penitent between his own legs, he had dropped his trousers, and his hands held the monstrous rope. Sitting in this position he murmured some words which I could not understand.

He lingered for some time in this devotional position and inspected the altar with glowing eyes. He seemed to be undecided how to effect his sacrifice, since there were two inviting openings. His eyes devoured both and it seemed as if he were unable to make up his mind. The top one was a well-known delight for a priest but, after all, he had also promised a taste of Heaven to his penitent. What was he to do? Several times he knocked with the tip of his tool at the gate he desired most, but finally he was smart enough to let wisdom triumph over desire. I must do him justice: I clearly saw his monstrous prick disappear the natural way, after his priestly fingers had carefully parted the rosy lips of Eradice's lovepit.

The labour started with three forceful shoves which made him enter about halfway. And suddenly the seeming calmness of the priest changed into some sort of fury. My God, what a change! Imagine, my dear count, a satyr. Mouth half-open, lips foam-flecked, teeth gnashing and snorting like a bull who is about to attack a cud-chewing cow. His hands were only half an inch away from Eradice's full behind. I could see that he did not dare to lean upon them. His spread fingers were spasming; they looked like the feet of a fried capon. His head was bowed and his eyes stared at the so-called relic. He measured his shoving very carefully, seeing to it that he never left her lovepit and also that his belly never touched her arse. He did not want his penitent to find out to whom the holy relic of Saint Francis was connected! What incredible presence of mind!

I could clearly see that about an inch of the holy tool constantly remained on the outside and never took part in the festivities. I could see that with every backward movement of the priest the red lips of Miss Eradice's love-nest opened and I remember clearly that the vivid pink colour was a most charming sight. However, whenever the good priest shoved forward, the lips closed and I could only see the finely curled hairs which covered them. They clamped around the priestly tool so firmly that it seemed as if they had devoured the holy arrow. It looked for all the world like both of them were connected to Saint Francis' relic and it was hard to guess which one of the two persons was the true possessor of this holy tool.

What a sight, my dear Count, especially for a young girl who knew nothing about these secrets. The most amazing thoughts ran through my head, but they all were rather vague and I could not find proper words for them. I only remember that I wanted to throw myself at least twenty times at the feet of this famous father confessor and beg him to exorcize me the same way he was blessing my dear friend. Was this piety? Or carnal desire? Even today I could not tell you for certain.

But, let's go back to our devout couple! The movements of the priest quickened; he was barely able to keep his balance. His body formed an 'S' from head to toe whose frontal bulge moved rapidly back and forth in a horizontal line.

'Is your spirit receiving any satisfaction, my dear little saint?' he asked with a deep sigh. 'I, myself, can see Heaven open up. God's infinite mercy is about to remove me from this vale of tears. I . . .'

'Oh, venerable Father,' exclaimed Eradice, 'I cannot describe the delights that are flowing through me! Oh, yes, yes, I experience Heavenly bliss. I can feel how my spirit is being liberated from all earthly desires. Please, please, dearest Father, exorcize every last impurity remaining upon my tainted soul. I can see . . . the angels of God . . . push stronger . . . ooh . . . shove the holy relic deeper . . . deeper. Please, dearest Father, shove it as hard as you can . . . Oooh! . . . ooh!!! Dearest Holy Saint Francis . . . Oooh, good saint . . . please, don't leave me in the hour of my greatest need . . . I feel your relic . . . it is sooo good . . . your . . . holy . . . relic . . . I can't hold it any longer . . . I am . . . dying!'

The priest also felt his climax approach. He shoved, slammed, snorted and groaned. Eradice's last remark was for him the signal to stop and pull out. I saw the proud snake. It had become very meek and small. It crawled out of its hole, foam-covered, with hanging head.

Everything disappeared back into the trousers; the priest dropped his dowl over it all and staggered back to his prayer stool. He knelt down, pretended to be in deep communication with his Lord, and ordered his penitent to stand up, cover herself and sit down next to him to thank God for His Infinite mercy which she had just received from Him.

What else shall I tell you my dear count? Dirrag left, Eradice opened the door to the alcove and embraced me, crying out, 'Oh, my dearest Therese. Partake of my joy and delight. Yes, yes, today I have seen paradise. I have shared the delights of the angels. The incredible joy, my dearest friend, the incomparable price for but one moment of pain! Thanks to the holy rope of Saint Francis my soul almost left its earthly vessel. You have seen how my good father confessor introduced the relic into me. I swear that I could feel it touch my heart. Just a little bit deeper and I would have joined the saints in paradise!'

Eradice told me a thousand other things, and her tone of voice, her enthusiasm about the incredible delights she had enjoyed left no doubt in my mind about their reality. I was so excited that I was barely able to answer her. I did not congratulate her, because I was unable to talk. My heart pounded in wild excitement. I embraced her, and left.

So many thoughts are racing through my mind right now that I hardly know where to begin. It is terrifying to realize how the most honourable convictions of our society are being misused. How positively fiendish was the way in which this cowl-bearer perverted the piety of his penitent to his own lecherous desires. He needled her imagination, artfully using her desire to become a saint; he convinced her that she would be able to succeed, if she separated her mind from her body. This, however, could only be achieved by means of flagellation. Most likely it was the hypocrite himself who needed this stimulation to repair the weakened elasticity of his flagging member. And then he tells her, 'If your devotion is perfect, you shall not be able to feel, hear, or see anything!'

That way he made sure that she would not turn around and see his shameless desire. The blows of the rod upon her buttocks not only increased the feeling in that part which he intended to attack, but they also served to make him more horny than he already was. And the relic of Saint Francis which he shoved into the body of his innocent penitent to chase away impurities which were still clinging to her soul, enabled him to enjoy his desires without any danger to himself. His newly-initiated penitent mistook her most voluptuous outburst of carnal climax for a divinely inspired, purely spiritual ecstasy.

All Europe has heard the history of Father Dirrag and Miss Eradice; the whole world has talked about it, but only a very few know about the true circumstances which led to the quarrel between the Jansenists and the Molinists. I won't repeat everything that has been said about this whole affair. You know the entire sordid story. You have read the pamphlets that have been distributed by both factions and you know the results of the whole process and the fights that ensued. Whatever little I know from my own experience, I shall tell you now.

Miss Eradice is about my age. She was born in the city of Volno and she is the daughter of a merchant. My mother moved in with him when we came to live in that town after my dear father passed away. Eradice has a beautiful figure, her skin is extraordinarily beautiful and has a snowy complexion. Her hair is black as ebony and her beautiful eyes make her look like the Madonna. We were playmates when we were children, but I lost contact with her when mother put me in the convent. Her main interest was to be better than her friends and excel in everything she undertook. This peculiar passion made her select piety, since this is the easiest way to reach a goal. She loved God as if He were her lover. When I met her again she had become Father Dirrag's penitent and all she could talk about were pious thoughts, retreats and fiery prayers. This was, at that time, quite a fad with this particular mystical sect in the provinces. Her virtuous demeanor had already given her quite a reputation for saintliness. Eradice had a good mind but she used it only to satisfy her desire to become capable of performing miracles. Everything which claimed to make this possible became for her unquestionable truth. That's the weakness of us poor, ignorant people. Our ruling passion − and everyone of us has one − absorbs all the others. We act only upon whatever satisfies that one passion, and everything that contradicts it is instantly dismissed from our minds. Thus we are never bothered by little facts which could so easily destroy our comfortable illusion.

Father Dirrag came from the village of Lode. At that time he must have been about thirty-three years old. He had a face like our painters use when they want to portray a lustful satyr, but despite the incredible ugliness, his features conveyed a powerful, irresistible spirit. His eyes were lustful and shameless. But his actions only indicated his concern for the souls of his flock, and his devotion to the greater glory of God. He was an extremely talented preacher, his speeches were friendly and unctuous. He

possessed the gift of persuasion. And he spent his entire
inborn shrewdness to achieve the reputation of God's
favourite Evangelist. And indeed, an incredible number
of women and girls from the best of society have done
penitence under his skillful direction.

As you can see, my friend, the good father and Miss
Eradice had a lot in common. Their characters and their
goals were so basically similar that it was almost
impossible for them not to get together. As soon as Father
Dirrag arrived in the city of Volno, where his reputation
had preceded him, Eradice veritably threw herself into
his arms. And they had barely come to know each other
when one recognized in the other the perfect instrument
to achieve the great goals of perfection and fame. I am
quite sure that Eradice initially acted in good faith, but
Dirrag knew exactly what he had bagged. The beautiful
face of his new penitent had captivated him and he knew
that he could easily lead her astray. He knew that he
would have no trouble at all in swindling this softhearted,
prejudiced, basically innocent girl who had a mind which
willingly and with full conviction soaked up his mystical
insinuations and admonitions. That was the framework
of his plan whose execution I have just described to you.
This plan promised him a whole series of voluptuous
entertainments long before he had reached his goal,
especially the act of flagellation. The good priest had used
those exercises already upon several others of his
penitents, but his lecherous actions had never gone
further. But the firm flesh, the beautiful figure and the
immense white buttocks of Eradice had heated his
imagination so much that he decided to take this last
important step.

Great men can overcome great obstacles. This priest
invented the intromission of a piece of robe which had

girded the waist of the holy Saint Francis. This relic was supposed to expel all the impurities of the soul and the last carnal thoughts which were still plaguing the members of his flock. It was also supposed to cause divine ecstasy. At the same time he also invented the stigmata with which the holy Saint Francis had been afflicted. In deep secret he invited one of his former penitents to come to Volno. This woman possessed his full confidence, especially since she had played the role voluntarily and knowingly which he now intended to play with Eradice. But he had found her too young and too full of enthusiasm about the possibilities of performing miracles. He did not dare make her his confidante and decided to play a trick upon her rather than reveal his secrets.

The old penitent arrived and soon this bigoted woman became as well-acquainted with Eradice as her fellow-devotee. It was the old girl friend of Father Dirrag who managed to fill Eradice's mind with the special devotion to the holy Saint Francis. The priest had given her a liquid to create a phony stigma. The old bigoted penitent washed Eradice's feet that next Maundy Thursday and used the occasion to apply some of the fluid, which immediately did its job.

A few days later Eradice took the old woman into her confidence and told her that she had a wound on each foot.

'Oh, what happiness! The miracle of it! And the fame for you!' exclaimed the old hypocrite. 'Saint Francis has imparted his most holy stigmata to you, his handmaiden! God surely intends to make a great saint out of you. Let's find out if you don't have the stigma on the side, like all great and venerable saints.'

And her hand touched Eradice under the left breast, quickly applying some of the acid liquid. And sure enough, the next day there it was . . . a brand new stigma.

Obviously Eradice talked to her father confessor about the miracle, but he wanted to avoid unnecessary publicity and advised the girl to be humble about it and keep the entire affair a deep secret. To no avail; the main passion of our poor girl was her incredible vanity and her desire to become a great saint. She was totally incapable of keeping the signs of her belonging to the chosen few from her friends and she began to make all sorts of confessions. Her stigmata caused considerable consternation and soon all the penitents of Father Dirrag wanted to have a stigma of their very own.

Dirrag understood the necessity to keep his fame and to divert the attention of his flock from Miss Eradice. A few penitents received the same stigmata and everything went along fine again.

Meanwhile, Eradice devoted her entire being to the holy Saint Francis and her father confessor assured her that he had the utmost confidence in the miraculous powers of that particular saint. He himself had performed many a miracle through a section of the rope of his holy man. A priest from his order had brought it with him from the Holy Father in Rome. With the help of this relic he had exorcized many a devil from some poor possessed soul, either by sticking it into the mouth of the victim or by penetrating another body opening. Finally he showed her the so-called rope. In reality this was nothing but a ten-inch long piece of hemp which had been soaked in tar to make it smooth and slick. He displayed it to her in a case, covered with purple velvet. Eradice, who was too innocent to know this, begged the priest for permission to kiss the instrument. He had told her that she would have to reach a state of utter humbleness, because any touching by profane hands would be a great and mortal sin in the eyes of the Lord.

This is how, my dear count, Father Dirrag succeeded in allowing his young penitent to endure for many months his lecherous embraces. And all that time she firmly believed she was enjoying the purely spiritual ecstasies of Heavenly grace.

She told me everything after the sentencing at that notorious trial. She confided to me that a certain monk – one who had played a great role in this whole unpalatable affair – had finally opened her eyes to reality. He was young, very handsome, strong, and passionately in love with her. He was also a friend of the family and therefore dined with her frequently. She became confidential, and the monk exposed the brazen Dirrag. From what she told me, it was rather obvious that she had no doubt whatsoever what took place during the embraces of her friendly monk. She gave herself to him out of her own free will. It seems that his behaviour did not do any harm to the reputation of his order but that may have been because he was young, strong and handsome. He doubled the exercises to twice weekly and his new convert felt so richly rewarded that she began to neglect the weekly devotional sessions with the old druid.

After Eradice had began to enjoy the wonderful effects of the natural member of the young monk and she realized that she had been cheated with this so-called rope, she felt grossly disappointed. Not only that, but her vanity had been hurt and she decided to revenge herself. She started the entire proceeding which is well-known to you and she was assisted by the passionate young monk, who was not solely interested in his party, but furious at the old Dirrag who had received so many favours from his beloved Eradice by playing tricks upon her innocence.

After all, in the opinion of the young, strong and handsome monk, Eradice was created only for his pleasure. The priest had clearly committed theft and he had to be punished spectacularly. His rival had to be burned! Only this could satisfy his injured feelings.

As I already told you, I went straight home as soon as Father Dirrag had left my girl friend's house. I had barely reached my little room when I threw myself down upon my knees, begging God for the grace to be treated like Miss Eradice. My mind was in a turmoil which had reached the proportions of near-insanity. An inner fire consumed me. I sat down, then I stood up, again I threw myself upon my knees, but I went nearly out of my mind, regardless of the position I was in. I threw myself upon my bed; the deep penetration of that red snake into the private parts of my girl friend had burned itself into my mind's eyes. It did not occur to me to think of carnal pleasures. I did not connect what I had witnessed in any way with voluptuous pleasure, any more than I realized the criminality of what I had just witnessed. Finally I trailed away in a deep slumber and I dreamed that the member of Father Dirrag had left his body and was now in the process of penetrating me.

Half asleep I took the same position which I had observed from Eradice and, still half asleep, I backed up, crawling on my belly till the bedpost was in between my legs and touched that part of me which itched, driving me out of my mind. The contact with the bedpost caused a sharp pain which woke me out of my reverie without diminishing that infernal itch. To free myself from the position which I had taken up, I had to lift my behind. Rubbing against the bedpost was unavoidable and it caused a rather peculiar tickling. I moved once more, then again, and again. The effect was amazing. Suddenly I was caught in a frenzy. Without really having any particular thought in mind I began to pump my behind against the bedpost. Finally I rubbed my private parts with incredible speed against the beneficient bedpost. And soon a delightful feeling came over me; I lost consciousness and sank into a deep, relaxing sleep.

A few hours later I woke up, clamping my beloved bedpost between my thighs. I was on my belly, and my behind was naked. I was quite surprised about this peculiar position because I had forgotten what had happened. In a similar way a dream disappears at the moment of awakening. I had quieted down considerably; the release of those divine juices had freed my mind of its obsession. I began to think about what I had seen at Eradice's home, and I tried to remember exactly what I had done. However, I failed to realize any connection. I could make no sense out of what had happened to me. The part which I had rubbed against the bedpost hurt awfully, and the insides of my thighs were sore. Despite the firm warnings of my former father confessor from the convent, I gathered all my courage and dared to look at that part of my body which was giving me so much pain. I could not bring myself to touch it, the terrifying threats of hellfire and brimstone were too firmly implanted in my mind.

Just when I had finished my inspection, our maid entered my room and announced that Madame Catherine and the abbot had arrived to take dinner with us and mother had ordered me to come downstairs and keep them company. I went downstairs.

It had been quite some time since I had seen Madame Catherine. Though she had befriended my mother, who had done her a few great favours, and though she was considered to be a very devout woman, I had not visited her for a long time, because I did not want to incur the displeasure of my father confessor. She made no bones about the fact she abhorred the principles and the mystical exhortations of Father Dirrag. And this venerable priest in turn was very firm about his opponents: he did not allow any member of his flock to associate with the penitents of other father confessors, his competitors. Without doubt he feared confidential exchanges and therefore enlightenment. Anyhow, it was an absolute condition which the venerable Dirrag extracted from all his penitents and one which they carefully kept.

We sat down to dinner. The meal was very pleasant and I felt a lot better than usual. My usual dullness had made place for a certain vivaciousness; the pains in my back had disappeared, and I felt as if I had been reborn. None of our neighbours were slandered during the dinner conversation, although this is usually the case when priests and pious women dine together. The abbot, who is a very bright man and who has travelled a lot, told us many an amusing story without harming anyone's reputation, at least not anyone we knew personally. We were all in a very good mood.

After we drank our champagne and had taken our coffee, my mother took me aside and berated me about not having visited Madame Catherine for such a long time.

'She is a darling lady,' said my mother, 'and one of my best friends. It is because of her that I enjoy such a good reputation in this town. Her virtue and her enlightened knowledge are proverbial, and she is revered by all who know her. We need her assistance and it is therefore my wish, nay, my express order, Therese, that you do everything in your power to acquire her friendship.'

I answered mother that she did not have to be afraid and that I would do everything I could to make Madame Catherine like me. Oh, the poor woman. She had no idea about the lessons I was to receive from this woman who had such a splendid reputation in our small home town.

Mother and I returned to our company. A few moments later I told Madame Catherine that I was terribly sorry for having neglected her for so long. I asked her to forgive me and to allow me one of these days to exlain to her why I had been so thoughtless. I would be more than happy to tell her in detail what had kept me from visiting such a good friend. But Madame Catherine did not let me finish and said with a sweet smile, 'I know everything you want to tell me, my dear. This is neither the time nor the place to talk about it. Every person is convinced he has his own good reasons and it is quite possible that they are right. One thing is certain it would be a pleasure to have you visit me and to prove this to you.' She continued, raising her voice slightly, 'I invite you here and now to have a late supper with me at my home. Is that all right with you?' she asked my mother. 'Obviously I expect you and the reverend abbot, too. Both of you have things to talk over, so Miss Therese and I are going out for a stroll; you know when and where we shall meet.'

Mother was delighted. Neither the principles nor the behaviour of Father Dirrag met with her approval and she hoped that the good advice of Madame Catherine would help me to swear off my inclination to mortification of the flesh, for which she held my father confessor directly responsible.

The possibility exists that Madame Catherine and my mother had made some secret agreement. If that was true, my mother's wishes were fulfilled very soon and far beyond her wildest expectations.

Madame Catherine and I left the house, but I had barely walked a hundred steps when a terrible pain tore through my body. I was incapable of standing up straight and Madame Catherine asked, 'But my dearest Therese, what on earth is the matter? Don't you feel well?'

Though I told her that it was nothing, she asked me a thousand questions. Women are curious by nature and her questioning was very embarrassing to me. This, obviously, did not escape her attention.

'Don't tell me,' she said, 'that you, too, belong to the stigmatized females of this town. You are not even able to stand up straight. You are beside yourself! Come into my garden, dear child, and recuperate. Let us sit down and wait till you feel better.'

The gardens of Madame Catherine were in the neighbourhood. We walked over there slowly and sat down in a delightful little summer-house close to the lake.

After some idle talk about common generalities, Madame Catherine asked me again if I really had stigmata, and how I felt under the spiritual direction of Father Dirrag. 'I am very sorry, my dear,' she said, 'but I cannot deny that this particular kind of miracle surprises me terribly, and I am dying to see some of these miraculous wounds with my own eyes. I have a fervent desire to convince myself of their existence. Oh, please, my dear child, don't refuse me my wish. Tell me where and how and when these wounds appeared. You can be very sure that I shall not misuse your confidence and I believe that you know me well enough to be convinced that I speak the truth.'

Not only are women curious, they also love to talk. I myself suffered from this little fault of my sex, and morever, several glasses of champagne had loosened my tongue. I was in pain and needed no prodding to talk at length. I decided to tell her everything. Of course, I had to admit to her immediately that I was not fortunate enough to belong to the select group of brides of God, but that I had witnessed the sacred wounds of Miss Eradice that very morning and that the venerable Father Dirrag had inspected them himself when I was there. A little more artful prodding from Madame Catherine caused me to tell her slowly, bit by bit, everything I had seen and heard that morning. Not only what I had witnessed at Eradice's home, but also what had happened in my own room. I told her that I suspected that the pain I suffered was a direct result of my rubbing the bedpost.

During this remarkable confession, Madame Catherine was smart enough not to show the slightest surprise. She nodded her agreement with everything I said and caused me therefore to tell her every single little detail. Whenever I became confused because I did not know the proper words to describe what I had seen or felt, she asked me to describe the situations graphically. Undoubtedly, the lechery and voluptuousness of the situations, coming from a girl as young and innocent as I, must have been very funny to this worldly wise woman. Never before have such vile and obscene situations been described so seriously.

When I had finished my story, Madame Catherine seemed to be far away with her thoughts. I asked her several questions, but her answers were very vague and short. Finally she pulled herself together, and told me that the things she had just heard were very remarkable indeed and they deserved her full attention. She would tell me later what she thought about it, and what I should do. But first things first, and I had to get rid of that pain.

She advised me to bathe the spot with warm wine, especially between my thighs which had been chafed by the bedpost.

'Be very careful, my dearest child,' she said to me. 'Don't tell any of what you have told me to someone else. Not even to your own mother and especially not to Father Dirrag. You have done something good and you have seen something evil. Come and see me tomorrow morning around nine o'clock, and I will be able to give you some better advice. You can count upon my friendship. Your noble character is quite obvious. Well, I see your mother. Let's go and meet her, and talk about something else.'

About fifteen minutes later the abbot arrived also. Late supper, as they call it in the provinces, actually is rather early. It was barely seven-thirty when food was served and we sat down to supper.

In between courses Madame Catherine could not help herself, and she made some rather satirical remarks about the good Father Dirrag. The abbot seemed to be quite surprised and he scolded her gently. 'Why,' said he, 'shouldn't everyone behave himself exactly as he deems proper and correct, as long as it does not violate the concepts of proper society? And so far we have not seen Father Dirrag breech propriety. I therefore beg you, Madame, to allow me to disagree with your remarks, till the opinion you have about my confrere is substantiated by facts.'

To prevent a direct answer. Madame Catherine artfully guided the conversation in another direction. Around ten o'clock we got up from the table; Madame Catherine whispered something into the abbot's ear, he nodded, and escorted mother and me to our home.

To understand my story you should know, my dear count, who Madame Catherine and the abbot are. I will therefore interrupt my tale and give you some idea of their backgrounds.

Madame Catherine is a member of a noble family. Her parents had married her off to an old naval officer of about sixty when she was only fifteen years old. The man died five years after the wedding, leaving his young widow pregnant with a boy. The birth of this child almost killed the mother and three months later the baby died. Through her son's death, Madame Catherine inherited a substantial fortune. The beautiful widow, barely twenty years old, was besieged by matrimonial offers from bachelors all over the country. But she was now her own mistress and made no bones about it that she enjoyed her new position and that she had no intention of ever again running the risk of dying in childbed. It was only a miracle, she said, that she had remained alive; she intended to keep it that way, and she was so firm about it that soon even her most ardent admirers lost courage and left her alone.

Madame Catherine had a marvellous mind; she was very firm in her opinions, but she did not form them unless she had subjected them to many tests. She read a lot, and enjoyed conversation, especially about philosophical and abstract matters. Her behaviour was beyond reproach. She was a true friend and she would offer assistance whenever she found an opportunity. My mother, for one, knew this out of her own experience. At the time I am talking about, Madame Catherine must have been close to twenty-seven years old. I will have more than sufficient opportunity to describe her physical charms later.

The abbot, who was a very dear and special friend and at the same time spiritual advisor to Madame Catherine, was a truly deserving gentleman. He was around forty-five years old, small but well-built, and had an open, very intelligent face. He carefully observed the demands required by his station in life and the high society whose advisor he was, loved him and lavished its attention upon him. He was very intelligent and his knowledge was remarkable. These qualities made him excellent for the high position he held in Volno and though I am very sorry, I am not at liberty to reveal its nature without giving away the abbot's true identity. He was the father confessor and true friend of many respectable and noble people, in the same way that Father Dirrag was father confessor to every bigoted, hysterical old maid, the professional devout female and an assorted bunch of fanatical bitches.

That next morning I returned to Madame Catherine's home at the appointed hour.

'Well, my dearest Therese,' she called out at the front door, 'how is my sore little friend? Did you sleep well?'

'I feel a lot better, my dear Madame,' I answered truthfully. 'I have done exactly what you told me. I have thoroughly bathed the sore parts in warm wine and it has relieved me tremendously. I only pray that the Lord will have mercy upon me and not doom me to the deep pit of fire in hell.'

Madame Catherine smiled; she poured me a small cup of coffee and said, 'What you told me last night is far more important than you could possibly believe. I have become convinced that it is imperative to talk to the abbot about it. He is waiting for you at this very moment in his confessional. I want you to visit him and to repeat to him, word for word, everything you told me last night. He is a man of honour, and I am sure that he will give you proper advice. You need that very badly. I also believe that he will give you a few new rules to follow, and if you are as smart as I think you are, you would do well to follow them! It is imperative not only for the well-being of your immortal soul, but also for your own good health. Your dear mother would die of misery if she ever found out what you have seen at the home of your girl friend Eradice. If she ever found out what I know, she would have a stroke. I cannot hide from you the fact that what you have witnessed at Eradice's was horrible. Now, go with God, my dearest Therese. Take the abbot into your confidence. I assure you that you will be very glad if you do.'

I burst into tears and left her home, trembling all over. I arrived at the abbot's mansion and, as soon as he saw me, he went into the confessional.

I did not leave out the tiniest detail. He listened patiently and with full attention till I had finished my entire story. He only interrupted here and there to ask for an explanation about a few things that did not seem quite clear to him.

When I had finished he said, 'You have made quite remarkable observations. Father Dirrag is a swindler, an unhappy soul who allows himself to be torn down by the strength of his passions. He is inviting his own doom and, worse, he will take Eradice along in his fall. And you, Miss Therese, are more to be pitied than to be scolded. We do not always have the strength to resist temptations. The happiness and unhappiness of our lives are quite frequently decided by chance, or, if you prefer, by good or bad opportunities. I advise you to avoid the bad opportunities. Cease all contact with Father Dirrag and his penitents but do not speak evil about them; God in his infinite love for His children, would not like that. I also advise you to visit Madame Catherine quite frequently. She means very well and she will be able to give you lots of good, solid advice. It would indeed be a lot better for you if you tried to follow her example.

'And now, my child, we shall have to talk about that unendurable itching which you often notice in those parts of your body which you have been rubbing against the bedpost. That itching indicates certain needs of your temperament which are as important as eating and drinking. It is not necessary to encourage directly these certain needs but it would be foolish to deny their existence. If they are bothering you too much, there is absolutely nothing wrong in the eyes of God our Father in you bringing relief to that certain part of your body by rubbing it vigorously with a finger. I absolutely forbid you to stick your finger into the small hole you will find there. All you need to know now is that the husband, whom I am sure you will find one of these days, might get the wrong impression. But otherwise, I cannot repeat this too often, it is a feeling which Nature has implanted in us, and it is necessary to release the tensions which it creates at times. And Mother Nature also gave us a hand with fingers to satisfy the needs of our body.

'And, since we are nowadays convinced that the laws of Nature are also created by God, we cannot insult our Creator by not using the things He has given us to satisfy the needs whose impulses were His gift to us. Especially since by doing so the prurient interests of society are not disturbed if we only remain discreet about it. It is something entirely different, my dear daughter, to what has occured between the hypocritical priest Dirrag and his penitent Miss Eradice. He has swindled her, endangered her by possibly making her the mother of his bastard, because the so-called relic of the holy Saint Francis was nothing else but the male member which is used to impregnate women. Therefore he is sinning against the law of Nature which commands us to love our neighbour like ourselves. And I ask you, is it Christian charity when a priest puts a girl like your friend Eradice in a position to lose her good reputation; and to dishonour her for the rest of her natural life?

'You have seen, my dear child, how the priest rammed his tool into your girl friend and how he moved it back and forth. The connection of these two body parts, which are created for procreation, is only permissible when a woman is married. To do it with an unmarried girl can cause misery for an entire family. It is against the rules of society and therefore reprehensible. As long as you are not bound by the sacrament of marriage, don't allow any man to do this to you, regardless of the position you take. The simple means I have just advised you will suffice to keep the desire in check and to dampen the fire which may be caused by the wish. This simple cure will soon heal your failing health and I assure you that your body will bloom forth in beauty. I do not doubt that then your beautiful face will call forth suitors by the dozens who will try to lead you astray. Beware of them, and be very careful in your selection of a final partner. Never forget the lesson I gave you today. That will be all. I expect to see you next week at the same time and do not forget that the secret of the confessional is as sacred to the penitent as it is to the confessor. I must warn you that it is a mortal sin in the eyes of God, if only the smallest detail is talked about to outsiders.'

I must admit that the prescriptions of my new father confessor delighted my soul. I recognized instinctively a true and Christian charity and I also realized the ridiculous sham of Father Dirrag's unctuous lectures which I had held, alas, so sacred for so long.

After I had contemplated the advice all day. I sat down

44

on the edge of my bed before I went to sleep. I wanted to wash the shafed, sore parts again with warm wine. I spread my thighs as wide as I possibly could and began to inspect those parts very carefully and intensely. I shoved the lips of my cunny to the side and started to look for the little hole into which I had see Father Dirrag shove home his enormous prick. I finally discovered the little orifice but I could not believe that it was the same. It seemed so tight and tiny! I tried to stick my finger into it when I suddenly remembered the abbot's warning. Quickly I pulled my finger back and traced the little slit. Suddenly I touched a little protuberance. A little quiver ran through my body. I touched it again, and the shudder became voluptuous delight. I started to rub this little knob and soon I had reached the peak of delight. What a happy discovery for a girl who possesses such a richly flowing spring of life's juices!

For almost six months I swam in a sea of sensual delights, carried by waves of orgasms and whirlpools of lasciviousness. My health had become perfect, my conscience was unruffled thanks to my new father confessor who gave sensible advice which was adjusted to human passions. I saw him regularly every Monday in the confessional and almost every day at the home of Madame Catherine. I spent a lot of time with this lovely lady. The darkness which had for so long engulfed my spirit had disappeared; it had become a habit to think rationally and to judge calmly. Father Dirrag and Miss Eradice had almost disappeared from my memories.

How perfect can mind and spirit be molded by example and regulations! If it is true that they do not give us anything, and that we carry the seeds of everything within ourselves, then it is at least sure that examples and regulations serve to develop these seeds. They are able to make us realize thoughts and feelings of which we are capable and which would have remained hidden from our consciousness if we had been without example or without rules and regulations.

Meanwhile, mother had carried on with my late father's wholesale business. The results were disastrous, she had more enormous debts, and she had extended too much credit to a merchant in Paris who was now threatened with bankruptcy. This would ruin my mother, too. After she had consulted her friends, she decided to undertake a voyage to our marvellous capital city. My sweet, lovely mother loved me too much to leave me at home. The trip might be prolonged for quite some time, and she could not stand the idea that we should be separated for an indeterminate period. She decided therefore that I would accompany her to Paris. Ah! the poor woman had no inkling that she would find a miserable end in Paris and that I would find the wellspring of my happiness in the arms of my count!

The decision was made and we were to undertake our voyage in a month's time. It was agreed that I would spend the remaining time of our stay in Volno at the little country home of Madame Catherine which was about a mile away from town. The abbot visited us regularly and slept quite frequently in the guest room whenever his duties in town allowed him to do so. Both he and Madame Catherine showered me with attentions; they were no longer afraid to make remarks in my presence which were rather revolutionary and to talk about subjects of morality, religion and metaphysics which were in flagrant contradiction to what I had been taught previously.

I had already noticed that Madame Catherine liked the way I thought and reasoned about certain subjects, and that she was delighted whenever she succeeded in changing my opinion about a certain subject. She always forced me to come up with undeniable proof whenever I maintained an opinion about something. It annoyed me occasionally to notice that the abbot sometimes shook his head as if to warn her not to go too far on certain subjects. This discovery hurt my pride. I decided to try everything in my power to find out what they were trying to hide from me. It had at the time not occurred to me that these two people could have more than intellectual ties which bound them together. But soon, I was fully enlightened. I will tell you about that in a moment.

You are now about to learn, my dear count, the source from which I have acquired my moral and metaphysical principles which you have so carefully developed. These principles have enlightened me about what we are in this world and what we have to fear in the next. I thank them for the peace of mind and a way of life whose entire delight is made up by you.

It was a beautiful summer. Madame Catherine had the habit of getting up at five in the morning to take a stroll in the little forest near the end of her property. I had also noticed that the abbot, whenever he stayed overnight with us, had the same habit. After about two hours they would return home, go to Madame's bedroom and come downstairs around ten o'clock for a second breakfast.

I decided one day to hide in the bushes in such a way that I could overhear their conversation. Since I had no idea that they were lovers, I also did not think that I would lose anything if I were not able to see them.

I looked the place over very carefully and decided to hide in a place which seemed perfect for what I had in mind.

During supper the conversation drifted toward the workings and products of Nature.

'But what is Nature?' asked Madame Catherine. 'Is it a particular creature? Isn't everything created by God? Could it be possible that Nature is a subservient deity?'

'It is really not very intelligent of you to talk in such a manner,' exclaimed the abbot, his eyes twinkling. 'I promise you that I will explain what we are supposed to think about the Mother of the race of Men when we make our early stroll tomorrow morning in the gardens. It is too late now to talk about such a heavy subject. Can't you see that Miss Therese is exhausted? A discussion like this would bore her to death. I advise you, my dearest ladies, to go to bed. I shall recite my prayers and then follow your example.'

We took the abbot's advice and retired to our rooms.

The next morning before sunrise, I hid myself in the bushes I had selected. They were behind some trees which were connected by trellises along which roses climbed, thus forming a charming natural summerhouse, decorated by a few benches and little statues. After I had impatiently waited for a full hour, my two heroes finally appeared and sat down upon the bench which I had hidden behind.

'Yes,' the abbot said when they walked into the little clearing, 'she becomes lovelier every day. Her breasts have developed so well that they would completely fill the hands of some honourable priest. And her eyes have a sparkle to them which betrays her vivaciousness and her passionate temperament. Because she is very passionate, our little Therese. Imagine, I have given her permission to relieve herself with her finger and would you believe that by now she uses this form of satisfaction at least twice a day? You must admit that I am almost as good a doctor as a father confessor. Not only have I cured her spirit and mind, I have also healed her body and brought it to bloom.'

'Oh, come on now, my darling,' exclaimed Madame Catherine, 'have you finally finished with your dear Therese! Did we come here to talk about her beautiful eyes and fiery temperament? I really believe, Mister Joker, that you are tempted to tell her that you will help her relieve her tensions. You know very well that I am not a jealous mistress, and I would instantly give you permission if I did not fear that it could land you in a lot of trouble. Therese is a very smart and intelligent young girl, but she is too innocent and does not know enough about the ways of the world. You simply cannot afford to take her into your confidence. I have noticed that she is very curious. It is very possible that she can be of great use to us, but we must be careful and willing to wait. She suffers from a few great faults. I have just enumerated them to you. If she did not have those, I would not hesitate for a single second, and I would personally invite her to share our delights. Because it is really ridiculous to be jealous of our best friends and to deny them their happiness, especially since it would not in the least diminish ours.'

'You are absolutely right,' said the abbot. 'Jealousy and envy are two passions which can do a lot of useless harm to people who cannot think intelligently. But there is a difference between envy and jealousy. Envy is a passion which is born into Mankind and it belongs to his nature. Little children in the cradle are already envious of other children when they see what they get. Through education we may be able to weaken the results of this passion with which Nature has endowed us. But is a different story altogether with jealousy. Jealousy is

related to the joys of love. It is a result of our vanity and
our prejudices. After all, we know of entire populations
where the men offer the guests the enjoyment of their
wives, in a manner very similar to that in which we offer
our honoured guests the best stock of our wine cellars.
A native caresses the lover who is enjoying his wife, and
all his acquaintances are envious of such a friendship.
They laud him, and they congratulate him. A Frenchman,
in a similar predicament, would make a long face, his
acquaintances would point him out and laugh at him. A
Persian would stab both his wife and her lover, and all
his friends would honour him for it.

'Consequently I do not believe that jealousy is one of
the passions which Nature has implanted in us. It is
fostered by education and by whatever the prejudice
might be of the society in which its victim is brought up.
A woman in Paris reads, and is told as a young girl, that
infidelity on the part of her lover is an insult to the
woman; a young man is assured that a mistress or a wife
who cheats a little bit on him, dishonours the lover or
the husband. They imbibe these ridiculous principles, in
a manner of speaking, with their mother's milk. Out of
it grows jealousy, the green monster which tortures
mankind with unspeakable suffering which in reality is
not worth bothering about.

'Nevertheless, we must make a distinction between
fickleness and infidelity. I am in love with the woman
who loves me; her character is sympathetic to me; her
beauty and her passion make me happy. She leaves me.
In this case the resulting pain is no longer caused by some
prejudice. It is justified. I lose something which was really
good and beautiful, I lose a delight to which I had become
accustomed and which I am not sure whether I will be
able to rediscover. But what is the meaning of a minor

infidelity? This can be caused by a temporary mood, a sudden passionate feeling, or sometimes gratefulness. One really shows little intelligence in worrying about something like that, a tempest in a teapot which has no meaning at all, neither good nor evil.'

'Aha!' Madame Catherine interrupted the abbot with a smile. 'Now I understand what you are leading up to. You are trying to tell me that you are not unwilling, out of the goodness of your heart, to give our little Therese a small lesson in voluptuous pleasures, to give her a little love enema which, as far as I am concerned, is neither good nor bad. Well, my dear abbot. That's all right with me. It's a pleasure, because I love both of you. The two of you will gain something, and I stand to lose nothing. Why did you expect any resistance from me? If I became excited you might rightfully conclude that I am only in love with myself, that I am merely interested in my personal satisfaction, and that I want to increase that at the expense of something which you could find somewhere else any time you wanted it. But that is far from the truth. The happiness which I have acquired has nothing to do with throwing your satisfaction away. You don't have to be afraid, my dearest friend, to come close to me without being able to nibble to your heart's content at the little pussy of our dear Therese. Personally I think that it would do the poor girl a lot of good. But I warn you, my dear friend, be very careful!'

'That is a lot of nonsense. I did not even think about the little Therese. I only wanted to explain to you the mechanism which Nature . . .'

'Oh, please, let's stop talking about that!' answered Madame Catherine. 'But now that you mention Nature, you remind me of something. You forgot to tell me, if I remember your promise correctly, exactly who and

what this so-called Mother Nature of yours really is.
Let me hear how good your explanation is because
you always insist that you can explain everything
rationally.'

'I will fulfill your wish,' answered the abbot, 'but, my
dearest love, you know what I need first. I've got to do
it now. My imagination is terribly excited. I am absolutely
useless. I can't think of anything else. My thoughts are
confused and everything is absorbed by this one single
thought. I have told you what I used to do when I studied
in Paris, and my thoughts were primarily absorbed with
reading and exact sciences. The moment I noticed the first
carnal desires I would instantly procure a girl. The same
way one gets himself a pot to piss in when the bladder
gets irritated. I would take her once or twice in a manner
which you unfortunately won't allow me to do. My mind
would be cleared, my spirit would be calm, and I could
go back to my studies. I maintain that every student, and
every statesman with an ounce of passion in him, should
use this kind of a cure. It is as necessary for the health
of the body as it is for the sanity of the mind. I will go
even further. I maintain that every honourable man who
knows his duties toward society, should use this method
to make sure that he does not forget his duties because
of undue excitement, or tempts the wife and daughters
of his best friend.'

But what should women and girls do? They have, as
you say, the same needs men have, because they are
created out of the same flesh. Alas, we cannot use the
same methods, maybe because of a false sense of
modesty, or the fear of slander and gossip, or an
unwanted child . . . No, my friend, all these possibilities
don't allow us to use the same means as men. And
besides, where would we be able to find men who are

instantly ready and willing to service us, like your little girls in Paris?'

'Listen, my darling. Women and girls are allowed to do what you do and what Therese is doing twice a day. And if this game does not really satisfy you (and I know that there are lots of women who don't really like it), then you always have the choice to use that fantastic invention which they call a dildo and which is a very satisfying copy of the real thing. And moreover, your imagination will help you with the rest. No, I still maintain that men and women are only allowed to find those satisfactions which do not disturb the order of society. But when women start to enjoy just about any delight that strikes their fancy, then they have to voluntarily bear the yoke which society puts on their shoulders. You may call this injustice, but it is an injustice which is for the greater good of society.'

'Aha, my poor abbot. Now you have really talked yourself into a fine mess. You are trying to tell me that a woman or a girl can enjoy a man whereas a man of honour cannot enjoy a woman. It would destroy the very fabric of your precious society if he were to try and lead an honourable female into temptation. But you, yourself, you little hypocrite, have tried on hundreds of different occasions to lead me astray and you would have succeeded a long time ago if I had not been so deadly afraid of pregnancy. So, you have acted against the welfare of society to satisfy your own little desires.'

'Well, we are back on our old theme again,' said the Abbot. 'It's always the same song, my little love. Haven't I told you a hundred times that there are certain precautions which make such an accident impossible? Haven't you, yourself, admitted that women should only be afraid of three things: the devil, the loss of reputation, and pregnancy? As far as the first is concerned, I'm quite sure that you are not worried. I also don't believe that you have to be afraid about the second point as far as I am concerned. Only a mistake from you could damage your good name. And thirdly, a woman can only become a mother through the stupidity of her lover. I have told you a thousand times that because of its very construction nothing is easier to avoid as far as a man's prick is concerned. And though I have told you so often, I will gladly repeat it once more.

'A lover can only get into the mood for screwing by two things: his own imagination, or the sight of his loved one. The flow of blood makes his prick thick and stiff. Since they both want to do it, they get into the proper position. The prick of the lover is shoved into the cunt of his mistress, and through mutual rubbing and pumping the juices are being prepared to flow out of the respective parts. The moment the jism is about to be expelled the wise lover who knows how to control his passions will pull the bird out of the nest and with his own hand, or the hand of his loved one, only a slight jerking is necessary to shoot the divine load. And there is absolutely no need to worry about being made pregnant.

'A lover who does not use his brains, or one who shoves it in too deeply and who cannot pull out of the cunt in time, he is the one who squirts his seed deep into the womb, and that is the spot where the child develops.

'That is the precise mechanical way of the enjoyment of love. You know me well enough. Could you truly believe that I belong to those I mentioned last? The ones that do not use their God-given intelligence? No, my dove. I can speak out of experience when I tell you that I have proof of the opposite a hundred times over. I implore you. Let me prove it to you now. Today. Look at the triumphant state of my little boy; you are holding it in your hand. Oh, please, squeeze a little bit harder. You see, he is begging for your mercy, and I . . .'

'No! Please, no! No, my dearest abbot!' exclaimed Madame Catherine. 'I beg of you, don't do it! No matter what you say, I cannot get over this horrible fear. I would give you an enjoyment of which it would be absolutely impossible for me to partake. And that would be terribly unfair. Allow me to bring sense to this fresh little one . . . Well,' she continued after several moments of silence, 'are you satisfied with my breasts and my thighs? Have you kissed and caressed them to your complete satisfaction? And why are you trying to shove my sleeves above my elbows? The gentleman undoubtedly enjoys the sight of a moving, naked arm. Am I doing all right? You don't say a word. Oh, you rascal! Look at the way he is enjoying himself!'

For a moment everything was quiet. Suddenly I heard the abbot exclaim. 'Oh, my dearest little one, I can't stand it. Please, hurry! Quick, quick . . . come, come . . . with your darling little tongue, aaa . . . it's . . . squirting!'

Imagine, dear count, the situation in which I found myself. I tried to get up at least twenty times to find some little opening in the bushes which would allow me to see what was going on. However, the rustling of the leaves prevented me from doing so. I sat upright and tried to stretch my neck as far as I could. A fire consumed me and I used my normal way to contain it. Extinguishing the flame had become quite impossible.

After a moment, during which he undoubtedly put his clothes in order, the abbot began to speak again. 'Really, my dearest. Come to think of it, I am afraid that you were right again. I am glad that you denied me the enjoyment I wanted because I am afraid that I would have lost my mind completely and I would never have pulled out in time. I felt such an enormous delight, and such a great ecstasy that I would have come right smack into your belly.'

'Yes! I know we are truly weak creatures and not very capable of controlling our desires. I know all that, my dearest abbot. You are not telling me anything new. But tell me, are we really not going against the interests of society by giving in to the enjoyments we just experienced? And those so-called intelligent lovers who are so careful in pulling the bird out of the nest, and who allow the juices of life to dribble away on the outside. Don't they commit a similar crime? Don't they rob society of a possible member who could have become very useful?'

'That sounds reasonable,' retorted the abbot, 'but you will see, my love, that your reasoning is rather superficial. There is neither a human, nor a divine law, which invites us, let alone forces us, to work on the multiplication of the human race. All the laws we have compel an immense amount of bachelors and maidens, as well as droves of filthy monks and useless nuns, to observe continence. They allow a married man to fuck his pregnant wife and you could hardly call that useful. He merely spends his jism in a place that needs it the least. As a matter of fact, being a virgin is considered more desirable than being a married woman.

'Don't you agree that those people who cheat a little while fucking, or those who enjoy licking a pussy, don't do anything more or less than all those monks and nuns, and all the other ones who remain unmarried. They keep their seed in balls that are basically as useless as those who come outside of a cunt. As far as society is concerned, they are in exactly the same position. Neither one of these groups contribute any new members to society. But our common sense tells us that it is a lot better to waste the seed and enjoy doing it, especially since it does not do anyone a bit of harm, than to keep it and save it at the expense of our health and sanity. So you see, Madame the philosopher, that our enjoyment does no more harm to our precious society than the accepted celibacy of monks, nuns and the whole rest that prefer to remain unmarried, and so we shall be able to continue our enjoyment just as we have always done.'

The following exclaimations left no doubt in my mind that the abbot was of the opinion that he had to offer certain services to Madame Catherine, because I heard her exclaim, 'Oh, please, don't do that, you naughty abbot! Get away with that finger. I am really not up to it today, I am still worn out from yesterday's playing around. So please, don't do it till tomorrow. And besides, you know very well that I like to do it in comfort. I prefer my soft bed over this hard, uncomfortable bench any time. Quick, stop it. All I want from you now is your explanation of Mother Nature. Well, big philosopher. I helped to clear your thoughts, didn't I? Now talk . . . I am listening.'

'You want to know about Mother Nature? That is simple. Soon you will know as much about her as I do. She is a creature who only exists in our imagination. She is nothing but the useless sounds of words. The first founders of religions and the first leaders of nations were at a complete loss to explain to their people the concepts of moral right and moral wrong. And therefore they invented a creature who stands between God and us. And then they made this creature the founder of our passions, the originator of our illnesses, the reason for our crimes. How else could they possibly have explained the infinite love and goodness of God? How could they have given a reasonable explanation for such human vices as murder, theft, treason and rape, just to name a few? Why are there so many illnesses and so much physical suffering? What has the poor cripple who is doomed to crawl in misery all his life done to incur God's wrath?

'A theologian gave us the simple answer to all those questions: It is the work of Nature. But, what and who is this Nature? Is it another God we don't know? Does it act all by itself, independently from the will of God? Oh no, the theologian will answer smugly. Since God is incapable of doing evil because of His infinite love, it follows that evil can only exist through Nature. − What incredible nonsense! Am I supposed to complain about the whip that is hitting me, or about the person who is wielding it? Because isn't he the one who causes the pain I feel?

'So why don't we simply want to admit that Nature is an empty word, a concept which has been created by our weak human intelligence? Why can't we admit that God is everything! That a physical suffering which may be harmless to one, can be beneficial for another. In other words, as far as God is concerned, there is no evil in the world. The things we call good or evil are only so in relation to their effects upon our society, not in relation to God through whose will we operate in the first place, following precisely the laws and principles which he has laid down at the time of creation. A person steals something. If he is successful, it is good as far as he is concerned, bad as far as his victim is concerned. If the victim is of value to society, the thief is very bad. But, I maintain, that from God's point of view, the thief is neither good, nor bad. He has been created a thief and fulfills his function. I must admit that the man may have to be punished, even though he has acted under compulsion, and I am convinced that he was not free to commit his crime or not commit it. But he has to be punished, because punishment of a person who has disturbed the mechanism of an orderly society is deemed necessary to prevent other criminals from doing the same thing. The punishment which the unfortunate law-breaker has to suffer is supposed to be for the common good of society which, in this case, must take precedence over the well-being of the individual.

'Actually, my dearest love, I presume that you now have an inkling of what I mean when I used the term, 'Mother Nature.' It is a meaningless invention, because we cannot stand the mere idea that God could not care less about the little doings of a handful of mere mortals. We have invented a system of morals where the Creator of the universe has been degraded to a village shopkeeper who is the confidant of all the gossipy housewives. For certain acts He is supposed to shake His head, for others to nod agreement and for a few He should arise indignantly. We have perverted our religion into a snooping system of bed manners, we have made our body into a temple of filth and the pleasures of the body into a sin. Finally we have decided that it cannot be the shopkeeper's fault, and we have invented Mother Nature who can take the blame, because only lowly peasants and total morons are still willing to believe in the devil. But that is another subject which I intend to discuss with you tomorrow morning. I will tell you precisely what I think of religion in general. It is a very important subject, especially since it concerns our happiness. But for today I have talked enough. I would love to sip a cup of hot chocolate.'

'That is fine with me,' said Madame Catherine, straightening her dress. 'My dear gentleman philosopher undoubtedly needs the physical strength of this heartening drink, especially since I have taken away a considerable amount of his procreative powers. You have been on your very best behaviour and told me some marvellous things. Your remarks about Nature were absolutely fantastic, but I am afraid that you won't be able to enlighten me in a similar manner on the subject of religion. Besides, how could you expect to convince me with proof about a subject which is largely based on belief?'

'We'll talk about that tomorrow,' answered the abbot.

'Fine, but don't think that I will let you get away with mere words. Tomorrow, with your permission, we shall retire early to my room, because I will need my comfortable bed and your caressing fingers . . .'

A moment later they walked back to the house. I followed them from a distance, slipped through the back door, and raced up to my room to change dresses. Then I walked downstairs to say good morning to Madame Catherine and the abbot who were already drinking their chocolate. I was afraid to stay too long in my own room, because the possibility existed that the abbot would start his conversation about religion anyway, and I did not want to miss a single word of it. His discourse about Nature had made a tremendous impression upon me. I saw now clearly that God and Nature were one and the same thing, or at least that it is Nature which carries out the will of God. I drew my own conclusions from that momentous discovery and I began to think, perhaps for the first time in my life.

I trembled when I walked into Madame Catherine's room. I felt as if she knew that I had spied upon her and the abbot, and I was incapable of hiding my excitement. The abbot looked at me carefully. I pretended not to notice it. But I heard him whisper to Madame Catherine, 'Look at our little Therese. Isn't she pretty! Her complexion is charming, her eyes sparkle and her face is twice as intelligent as it was yesterday.'

I don't know what Madame Catherine answered him, but they both smiled. I pretended as if I had heard nothing, and stayed with them all day like a devoted watchdog.

That night, when I had retired to my room, I developed my war plan for the next morning. I was so afraid that I would oversleep that I decided to stay awake all night. Around five in the morning I saw Madame Catherine hurry toward the little clearing where I knew that the abbot was awaiting her. After what I had heard the previous day I also knew that they would return soon to Madame Catherine's room with the enormous, comfortable bed. Without further ado I went into her room and hid behind the curtains at the head of the bed, leaning against the wall and making sure that I could shove the curtain slightly aside without making noise. I did not want to miss anything! They could not whisper the slightest word without me being able to pick it up. I waited for a long time and I began to become impatient. I was afraid that they had changed their minds and that my plans would fail. But finally the two heroes of the comedy, which I shall now describe, entered the room.

'Do it to me, my dear friend,' said Madame Catherine, leaning back on her bed. 'Your story about the evil painter of Chartreux has made my blood boil. His portraits are beautiful and very true to Nature; if they had not been so dirty the book would be a true classic of art. Stick it into me, my dearest abbot. Today I have decided to let you do it. I implore you! I am dying with wild desire and I am ready to bear the consequences!'

'Don't dream about it,' said the abbot. 'And I have two good reasons for it. In the first place, I love you and

I am too decent to gamble with your good reputation. Besides, I am sure that afterward you would accuse me of carelessness. And in the second place, as you know, the doctor is not always capable of performing his duties. Now, I am not a peasant . . .'

'All right, all right! That's enough!' Madame Catherine exclaimed impatiently. 'Your first reason was good enough and took too long to explain. I can't hold it much longer. But please, sit down here,' she continued with a voluptuously purring voice, stretching languidly out on the bed, 'and let's bring a little sacrifice, as you call it.'

'Ah! I would love nothing better, my dearest angel!' said the abbot. He stood up and carefully uncovered her breasts. Then he lifted her skirt and chemise to well above her navel, spread her thighs and lifted her knees a little, pushing her heels together.

In this position the abbot kissed every single part of the body of his loved one. Madame Catherine remained motionless, her eyes were closed, she groaned softly and it seemed as if she was dreaming about unspeakable delights yet to come. The tip of her tongue moved rapidly across her lips, her eyelids opened slowly and her eyes were glazed. Her rosy lip began to quiver and the muscles of her face began to twitch. She had reached a state of voluptuous excitement. 'Hurry up with your kisses,' she exclaimed. 'Can't you see that you are killing me. Stop it or start it . . . I can't stand this any longer!'

The agreeable father confessor did not have to be invited for a second time. He lowered himself on the bed, put his left hand under Madame Catherine's head and his lips touched hers. His tongue slid slowly into her mouth and slipped out again, sliding back and forth, licking her lips, her teeth, filling her mouth and sucking her tongue. Meanwhile his other hand turned to the main business. He caressed her with true artistry.

Madame Catherine's cunt was richly covered with black curls and it was here that the abbot's finger lingered and played his virtuoso game. I was in a marvellous position to see the entire procedure. The rich fleece of Madame Catherine was exactly in my field of vision. Under it I could see a large part of her behind which she was moving in a slow undulating motion, a sure sign of her inner turmoil. Her thighs, the most beautiful, firm, well-rounded thighs one can imagine, and her knees, were also in motion. They weaved slowly back and forth from left to right and vice versa. It seemed to contribute to her delight and the finger of the abbot, which had entirely disappeared in the black curls, followed every one of her moves.

It would be a rather fruitless attempt, my dear count, to try and tell you what I was thinking at that particular moment. I mechanically imitated everything I saw. My hand did the same to my own body that the abbot's deft fingers were performing on the lower belly of Madame Catherine; I even imitated every single movement my dear friend was making.

'Aah! I'm dying!' she exclaimed suddenly. 'Put it in, my dearest abbot . . . shove it in as deep as you can. Please, deeper . . . yes, I implore you, shove it up as hard as you can . . . shove it, push it, deeper, harder! Oooh, that feels good . . . the darling little one is doing his job well! Ooh, what delight . . . I am coming . . . it's flowing . . . I . . . I . . .'

I imitated everything I saw, and without thinking for a single moment about the warning of my father confessor, I pushed my finger up as high as I could. The stabbing pain did not prevent me. I pushed as deep and as hard as I could, and soon I reached my climax.

The excitement subsided and I almost fell asleep, despite the uncomfortable position in which I found myself. When I heard Madame Catherine approach the spot where I was hiding, I almost died of fear. But fortunately I remained undiscovered. She pulled the bell cord and sat down at the little table in the other corner of the room. Her servant brought two cups of chocolate, and while they slurped it quietly, they talked about the joys which they had just experienced.

'But why aren't you absolutely innocent?' asked Madame Catherine. 'You can tell me as often as you want that you do not encroach upon the rights of society, that we are driven by a need which for certain persons has to be treated like the satisfaction of thirst and hunger. You have proved to me beyond a shadow of a doubt that all our actions depend upon God's will, and that the concept of Nature is merely an empty word. But what is your honest opinion of religion? The only thing I know is that religion prohibits the extramarital delights of the flesh. Does that make religion an empty word, too? What? Have you already forgotten that we are not free to act? That all our actions are predestined? If we are not free, how can we possibly commit sins?'

'You seem to be determined to talk about religion. I have studied the subject for years and years and God knows that I have tried to unravel the many mysteries connected to it. I have come to the following conclusion: God is good. His goodness is for me a guarantee that He shall not want me to make a mistake if I am truly and whole-heartedly devoted to the search for truth. But I have to know if God really wants me to follow any particular cult. It is obvious that if God is just, I must be able to recognize the true cult. Otherwise God would be unjust because He has given me the intelligence with which to make correct deductions and decisions.

'When a true Christian is unwilling to search for proof that his religion is the correct one, rather than to accept this blindly on faith, why would that same Christian, for example, demand that a Mohammedan, who is equally convinced that he has the proper religion, come up with convincing proof? They both believe that God has revealed their religion to them. The one by Jesus Christ, and the other by Mohammed.

'Our belief exists only because certain people have told us that God has revealed certain truths. But other people have told other members of different religions exactly the same thing. So, who are we to believe? To find the truth, we have to devise certain tests. Because everything which has been thought out by people must be subservient to our intelligence.

'All the founders of religions, wherever they may be found on Earth, have claimed that God has revealed His eternal truth to them. Which one are we allowed to believe? We could, of course, start to investigate which one of those religions is the true one. However, we have been prejudiced in favour of the one which we have been brought up in. The first thing we have to force ourselves to do is to sacrifice all our prejudices to God, and then take the light of our intelligence and inspect every question that arises in our mind.

'I would like to mention that from the entire civilized world, at the most one-twentieth embraces the Roman Catholic religion. The inhabitants of the other parts of the world maintain that we idolize a human being, that we pray to a slice of bread; they insist that we commit idolatry, pray to humans, and they also maintain that the

Church fathers contradict each other in their writings. To them, this is absolute proof that our holy books are not inspired by God.

'All the changes in religion which have occurred since the time of Adam, and which have been brought about by Abraham, Moses, King Solomon, Jesus Christ, and later the Church fathers, are proof of the fact that religion is a human undertaking. God himself has never changed, because He is unchangeable.

'God is everywhere. Nevertheless the Scriptures tell us that God looked for Adam in Paradise and asked, 'Adam, where art thou?' They also tell us that God walked in the Garden of Eden and talked with the devil about Job. My reason tells me that God cannot be passionate, because he would have to be subject to something stronger than Himself. Nevertheless, the sixth chapter of Genesis tells us that God was sorry to have created mankind, and his revenge is not idle. In our Christian religion God is so weak that he is unable to make Man do his bidding. He punishes him with water, then with fire, and Man remains invariably the same. He inspires the prophets. Man does not change. He has only one Son. He sends Him down to earth, and sacrifices Him because He loves the world so much! And still, Man does not change. What a ridiculous weakling has the Christian religion made out of its God!

'Everyone admits that God knows everything that will happen in eternity. Out of this follows that the God who allowed us to be born, knew beforehand that we were totally doomed, and that we were born to be unhappy throughout our lives.

'Nevertheless, the Scriptures tell us that God sent the prophets to warn us and to admonish us to change our ways. But, the all-knowing God must have known that

Man would not change. It follows that the Scriptures themselves assume God to be a cheat. Does that make any sense to you? Is that in accord with your belief in God's infinite goodness?

'The all-powerful God has an opponent. The devil. Against God's will, the devil manages constantly to acquire about three-fourths of the souls of Mankind, the Mankind which God allegedly loved so much that he sacrificed His only begotten son! However, it seems to me that God couldn't care less about the fate of the majority of Mankind. Now, how stupid am I supposed to be to believe all this idiotic nonsense?

'According to the Christian faith we only commit sins because we are led into temptation. The tempter, we are told, is the devil. All God has to do is to destroy the devil. Since he obviously has not done that it follows that either He is too weak, or unwilling. If He is unwilling He is unjust, if He is too weak He cannot be God.

'A fairly large amount of the servants of the Roman Catholic Church maintain that God gives us orders. However, we are incapable of following those orders, unless we are graced by God's infinite mercy which He only bestowes upon those who have found favour in His eyes. Nevertheless, God punishes those who are incapable of following His orders. Don't you see the contradiction? The monstrous perversity of it all?

'Can you think of anything more miserable than the thought that God is vengeful, jealous, full of wrath? Can you imagine any more pitiful sight than a bunch of Roman Catholics, down upon their knees, praying to a bunch of saints? As if those saints, like God, were omnipresent? And what if those saints could read the hearts of these people and hear their voices?

'The ridiculous double-talk that we do everything to

the greater glory of God. Do you truly believe that God's infinite glory could be increased one iota by the thoughts and deeds of little mortals? Could they increase anything on Him? Isn't God complete unto Himself?

'How could people possibly start an idiotic belief which tells them that God is happier when they eat a herring instead of a chicken, onion soup instead of beef bouillon, fillet of sole instead of a steak? And especially that this God would throw them in hell for all eternity if they happen to prefer a simple slice of bacon on a specific day rather than an expensive filleted fish?

'Oh, the stupid people who believe that they are capable of offending God. Even a prince and a king, if they use their brains, are above being insulted. Your religion teaches you that God is an avenging God, but at the same time you are being told that vengeance is sinful. The contradiction. On one hand we are assured that forgiveness of an insult is a virtue, while on the other hand our entire concept of original sin, the eternal threat of hell, is God's revenge for an unintentional insult.

'We are being told that, if there is a God, we do need a cult. But nobody can deny that God existed before the world, and at that time a cult was obviously not needed. And since the creation of the world, this earth has crawled with all sorts of animals who are obviously not in need of a cult. Without people, there would still be a world, there would still be animals, there would still be a God, but there would be no cult. People suffer from the sickly delusion that God cannot do His work without their meager help! They judge the acts of God according to their own little deeds.

'The Christian religion gives us an entirely false picture of God. According to its teachings, our human justice is based on the justice of God. But, if we apply the rules of our human justice, we would have to condemn God for his vile actions, especially those against His own son, against Adam, against the multitude of populations who have never had a chance to learn about His existence, and – most important of all – against all those little innocent children who died before they were given the chance of being baptized.

'According to the teachings of Christianity, we have to strive for perfection. In the opinion of the saints and the fathers of the Church, virginity is more perfect than the married state. It follows therefore, clearly, that the Christian concept of perfection equals the total destruction of the human race in the shortest time possible, because if we were to follow the exhortations of our priest literally, it would not take more than sixty or eighty years and the human race would have vanished from the face of the earth. Could a religion like that, such an abominable perversion, truly be inspired by God?

'And, since I am mentioning it, can you imagine anything more stupid than the idea that priests, monks and nuns, total strangers, have to do our praying for us. A communication with God through others? Their concept of God is as if He was a king on a throne who has to be pacified by lackeys.

'What unbelievable nonsense is the idea that God caused us to be born so that we would do nothing that which is against our nature, and that we are doomed to be as miserable as we possibly can be! We are required to give up everything which can satisfy the passions and desires that God has planted into our being. No tyrant could be worse. In all mankind the fiend has not yet been born who follows us with such sickening vengeance from the moment that we are born till the day we die, with the added possibility of eternal torture in hell.

'To be a perfect Christian, one has to be ignorant, capable of blind faith, disdain all pleasures, give up joy, honour, riches, leave friends and family, and maintain virginity. In short, one is supposed to do everything which is against so-called Nature, while this same Nature has been ordained by God, and surely is part of His unalterable will. These unbelievable contradictions are supposed to belong to a Being which is all-knowing, all-just and all-good!'

'In my opinion, since God is the creator and master of all things, we are obliged to use our facilities for the purposes for which they have been created. We can try and find out those purposes with the intelligence and the feelings with which God has endowed us. It is our duty to find out His goal and purpose, and to bring that in accord with the goals and purposes of human society. Obviously Man has not been created to do nothing. He is supposed to do something which serves his own purposes and which does not damage society. God has not created a multitude of people just for the benefit of a few; He does not want the happiness of a single person, He wants the happiness of all. Therefore we are obliged to be of service to each other, provided that this does not damage one branch or the other of human society. If we keep this in mind, we will all do our duty towards God. The whole rest of the religious structure can then be summarily dismissed as pretentiousness and prejudice.

'All religions, without exception, are the work of men. There is not a single one that does not have its martyrs and saints who have allegedly performed miracles. What do the miracles of the Christian religion prove to me, if other religions claim the same miracles?

'In the first place, all religions are based on fear. Thunderstorms, snow and hail, and unbearable heat destroyed the fruits of early Man's labors. They were at an absolute loss to defend themselves against those forces of Nature, they were at their mercy, and consequently they assumed that there had to be a force stronger and more powerful than themselves. They assumed that these forces would be appeased by prayer and sacrifices, and that these 'gods' found a special delight in torturing defenseless people. In the course of the centuries, and in various countries, many people decided to organize those beliefs and form religions. They invented the most fantastic and incredible gods. They organized themselves into orders and societies whose members had to be subdued and kept in fear. They became their leaders, political as well as religious. They realized that they could only remain in business if they kept fear among their followers and ordered them to keep their passions in check. They also realized that mere exhortation was not enough, that they had to hold out rich rewards and horrible punishments. Only then can people be brought to obedience.

'These politicians invented our religions. Every single one of them promises rewards, and threatens punishments. This way they have induced the majority of Mankind to act against the natural impulses, passions and desires. Some of those passions, I must admit, are reprehensible. They include the desire to possess the neighbour's wife, or to rape his daughter. Among them are the impulse to wreak vengeance in a terrible manner, or to soil another's good reputation to make one's own questionable deeds seem less reprehensible by comparison. Some religions have even invented the concept of honour. There is nothing wrong with that in itself, because in general this is to the greater good of society and can, at times, be useful for the individual.

71

'I don't doubt the fact that there is a God Who has created everything and Who has set this universe in motion according to His own laws. Everything is therefore necessary and interlocking. There is no chance. The three dice which a player throws upon the table, will necessarily show a certain amount of eyes. The number of eyes depends upon the manner which the dice were shaken and the strength with which they were thrown. All the actions of our life can be compared with a game of dice. All our actions are a direct result of previous actions which, in turn, are a result of their previous actions. We can go back and forth into eternity.

'Therefore, when I am told that a person wants something because he desires it, I consider that a meaningless statement. Throughout our life we are forced to do something as it is dictated by the combination of our intellect, our passions and our own previous deeds. Life, indeed, is a game of dice.

'Let me assure you, my dearest friend, that I do believe that we should love God. Not because He desires us to do so, but because He is good. We should obey the human laws because those laws have been designed to protect the best interests of society. Since we are a part of that society, they are also in our own best interest.

'I have only told you this, because I consider you my best friend. This slight discourse is the result of twenty years of study, and thinking, and long, arduous, sleepless nights. I have tried to the best of my knowledge to separate wisdom from superstition, truth from lies. Let us therefore conclude, my dearest, that the joys we are giving each other are pure and innocent, they cannot insult God, and they do not insult society because we keep them secret. For all appearances we stick to the rules of propriety and the laws of men. If we were not to fulfill both conditions, I admit that we would excite the prurient interests. Our example could lead young and innocent people astray.'

'But,' protested Madame Catherine, 'if our pleasures are as innocent as you say, and I am inclined to believe you, why don't we go out and teach the world how to enjoy their pleasures? Why don't we tell our friends and acquaintances about the results of your metaphysical research and let them share our peace of mind and our happiness? Haven't you told me a hundred times that your greatest joy would be to make people happy?'

'Yes, I did. And I did not lie,' answered the abbot. 'But beware of telling the ignorant masses about self-evident truths. They don't feel it in their bones, and they would only misinterpret their meanings. Only those who know how to think intelligently, who understand the art of keeping their passions in balance, and who will not be brought down to their knees by others, are worthy of knowing the truth as I have come to understand it. But men and women of that caliber are a rarity. Among a hundred thousand of them, not twenty are capable of thinking, and of those twenty there may not be more than one capable of some original thought. Most of us will be swayed by our ruling passion. That is the main reason why we have to be exceedingly careful about voicing thoughts like the one we have been talking about this morning.

'Very few people understand the necessity of caring about the happiness of their fellow men as the only way to secure happiness for themselves. That is why it is dangerous to point out the inherent weakness of religions, because it is the only thing that forces them to care about others. The rules and regulations, no matter how silly and stupid the reasoning behind them, makes them work for the greater good of society, and therefore for themselves. Religions are a mere veil, the real incitements are the promises of eternal happiness and the threats of eternal damnation. These fears and hopes are the guiding forces for the weak, and their number is huge. Honour, justice and concern for the common good guides those who can think. Alas, their number is so small as to be almost negligible.'

The abbot fell silent. Madame Catherine thanked him in terms that left no doubt of her happiness. 'You are the most darling friend any woman could wish for,' she exclaimed, embracing the abbot with ardent fire. 'How lucky am I to be in love with a man who can think as clearly as you do. Be assured that I will never misuse your confidence in me, and I promise to follow your intelligent principles for the rest of my life.'

They exchanged kisses, lingering passionately in each other's arms. I was bored silly, especially since I was sitting in a very uncomfortable position. But finally my pious father confessor and his learned pupil went downstairs, and I ran to my room where I locked myself in securely. Only a few moments later the maid called out that Madame Catherine would enjoy the pleasure of my company. I told her that I begged Madame to be excused for a few more hours, since I had slept very badly that night. I spent the time writing down everything I had heard.

The days passed in pastoral tranquility. We became the best of friends. Suddenly, one day, my mother arrived, informing me that we had to depart the next day to Paris. We had dinner with Madame Catherine for the last time, and I said my farewells, crying hot tears. The darling woman caressed me, and gave me much good advice without making me feel inferior. Unfortunately the abbot

had gone to a nearby town, where his duties would keep
him for at least a week. I did not see him. Mother and
I returned to Volno where we spent the night. That next
morning we took the coach to Lyons and from there we
transferred to Paris.

As I already told you, my mother had decided to make
this trip, because a merchant in Paris owed her a
considerable amount of money. Mother's entire fortune
depended on his payment. She had enormous debts, and
business was bad. Before she left Volno, she had given
power of attorney to one of her distant relatives. This
man ruined us completely. One day, mother learned that
all our possessions, including the house in Volno, had
been sold to satisfy her distant cousin's gambling debts
and that same day she found out that the Parisian
merchant had gone bankrupt. This was too much for her.
Within a week she died of a brain fever.

There I was — alone in the big city with no friends,
no family, no one to take care of me but myself. I was,
as I had been frequently told, very pretty, I possessed
considerable knowledge but I had no practical experience.

Before her death, mother had handed me a purse with
four hundred gold pieces in it. Since I had plenty of linen
and clothes, I considered myself rich. Nevertheless, my
first thought was to enter a convent and become a nun.
Fortunately I gave up the idea when I remembered all
my previous misery and suffering with the nuns in Volno.
Besides, the woman who lived next door to me and with
whom I had a fleeting acquaintance, gave me very good
advice.

This woman, a certain Mrs Bois-Laurier, lived in a
furnished apartment adjoining mine in the same hotel.
She was kind enough to take care of me in the first weeks

after mother died, and she did not leave me out of her sight for one single moment. I was eternally grateful to her for that and felt very much obliged to her.

As you know yourself, Mrs Bois-Laurier was one of those unfortunate women who had been forced since early childhood to serve the bestial desires of the public. And, like so many others, she had assumed a different name when she could afford to live as a respectable woman. She had bought herself a pension with the earnings of her previous profession.

The mourning which consumed me those first few weeks gave way to some serious thinking. I began to get worried about my future. I confided in my new friend and told her about the bad financial state I was in, expressing my fears about my terrible predictament. But she had a healthy intelligence which had been strengthened by experience.

'Oh, you are so silly,' she told me one morning. 'Never fear about the future. The future is as unpredictable for the rich as it it for the poor. And you, my dear child, have no reason to worry at all. At least, far less than others. With your nice figure, your pretty face and clear complexion, with your intelligence and sparkling wit, a girl should never have to be afraid about the future. Especially not if she knows how to be smart. No, my dear, you don't have to be afraid. Leave everything to me, and I will find you what you need. I think you need a good husband, since you seem to be intent on doing it with the blessings of the sacrament. Oh, my dear child, you have no idea how dangerous such a wish can be. But, let me take care of it. A woman of forty with the experience of one of sixty knows precisely what a girl like you needs. I will take the place of your mother and I will introduce you to the possibilities of the great world. I shall introduce you tonight to my uncle, who is a rich man, a very decent man, and I am sure that he will find somene for you who deserves you.'

I threw my arms around Mrs Bois-Laurier's neck and thanked her profusely. I must admit that the soothing words had wiped away my fears, and I was convinced that from now on my future would be rosy.

How stupid can a girl be when she has a lot of confidence and absolutely no experience. The lessons of the good abbot had opened my eyes and I knew that we had to obey the laws of God and Man and I also knew that at times we could break the laws of Man when they were in contradiction with the laws of God. Not to be caught was the main concern. But, alas, I had no idea of the depths of human passion.

Everything I saw and heard seemed as justified as the ideas of Madame Catherine and the abbot. I thought that the only villain in the world was that infamous priest, Father Dirrag. Oh, poor innocent girl! What an incredible mistake! The rich Mr Bois arrived that evening around five o'clock at the home of his niece. The first few hours of his visit were spent on something other than talking about my plight. The niece was, as she herself admitted, too clever to show me immediately to her uncle, because she did not want, as she put it, to upset him with the immediate view of my considerable charms. She wanted to talk to him alone and it was past seven o'clock when she called for me. I greeted him as demurely as I possibly could, but he seemingly did not deem it necessary to get up. He invited me to sit down upon the chair that was put beside his huge easy chair upon which he was half-sitting, half-reclining. His enormous belly was covered only by a shirt and his manner was like that of most financiers. Nevertheless, I thought he was a very nice man. He paid me many a compliment, including one about the firmness of my thighs. Suddenly he stretched out his pudgy hand and squeezed me so strongly that I cried out with pain.

'My niece has told me about you,' he said gruffly, without bothering about the pain he had caused me. 'Goddamn, what beautiful eyes. Marvellous teeth, and the firmest flesh I have felt in a long time. Oh, I promise you, we'll make something out of you. Tomorrow I will make an appointment for you with a colleague of mine. You shall meet him at dinnertime. The man veritably swims in gold, and if I know him as well as I think I do, I assure you that he'll instantly fall in love with you. Just be nice to him. He is a man of honour, and he will satisfy you completely. Well, children, it's getting late,' he added, buttoning his vest and hoisting himself out of the chair. 'Good night, my children, give me a kiss, and treat me as you would your own father. And you, dear niece,' he continued, 'see to it that she is on time in my pleasure home, and that there is enough to eat and drink for all.'

When the rich uncle had left, Mrs Bois-Laurier said to me, 'You can congratulate yourself, Therese. My uncle liked you very, very much. Sometimes his manners leave something to be desired, but he has a heart of pure gold. He is a true friend. You know how much I like you and therefore you must let me take care of all the little details. Just follow my advice to the letter, and I assure you that soon you will not have a worry in the world. One thing I must impress upon you: For God's sake, don't be a prude. That could ruin everything we are trying to do for you. Nobody ever makes a fortune if they are too prissy.'

I had dinner with my newfound protectress and she managed to find out all about my life, my thoughts and ideas with a very clever line of questioning.

She was very open and honest, and this caused me, too, to make many confessions. I talked much more than I really wanted, and it seemed that she was rather shocked to find out that I had never had a lover. However, she was quickly put at ease when I confessed to her that certain ways of love were not unknown to me and that I had already tasted a considerable amount of sexual satisfaction. She embraced me, kissed me and tried to do everything in her power to talk me into spending that night with her. However, I declined politely, went to my room, filled with joyful thoughts about my promising future.

The women of Paris are vivacious and helpful. That next morning, Mrs Bois-Laurier entered my room, woke me up and asked me if she could help me dress. She offered to curl my hair but, since I was still in mourning for my dear mother, I declined and kept my little bonnet on my head. Bois-Laurier was very curious and exceedingly prankish that day. She thoroughly examined all my charms with her eyes and her hands before she handed me my chemise. She insisted on helping me put it on. Suddenly a thought struck her, and she exclaimed, 'Wait a minute, you little rascal! You are putting on your chemise without having brushed your pussy! Where is your bidet?'

'I really don't know what you mean. What is a bidet?'

'What? No bidet? Don't let any of your suitor's hear that you don't have a girl's most important piece of furniture. My God, child, it's almost more important than a clean chemise. For today you can use mine, but tomorrow, it's got to be the first thing you will have to buy for yourself.'

Mrs Bois-Laurier's bidet was brought into my room; she made me sit down upon it and despite my violent protests she insisted on brushing my pussy. She used a lot of lavender water and I could not understand why she washed my private parts so thoroughly. But then, I did not have the vaguest idea of the big party she had planned for my pussy . . .

That afternoon we drove to the pleasure home of the uncle, which was situated outside the city. Uncle Bernard was already there when we arrived, together with his friend and colleague, a man of about thirty-eight to forty years old. He was reasonably handsome. His clothes were very expensive and he wore many rings, flashing the diamonds with seeming delight. His snuff box of pure gold, his gold watch on a heavy gold chain, and several other pieces of golden jewellery seemed to play an important part in his life. But he nevertheless deigned to walk toward me, take my hand in his and look me over very carefully. 'Goddammit, she is pretty!' he exclaimed. 'Upon my word, she is charming; I swear, I'll make her my little wife.'

'Oh, dear sir,' I stammered, 'you honour me greatly, and as soon as I no longer . . .'

'No, no,' he interrupted, 'don't you worry your pretty little head. I will take care of everything and I will see to it that you are totally satisfied.'

The servant announced that dinner was served. We sat down and I was pleased to know that Mrs Bois-Laurier knew what form of conversation was acceptable and usual in the better circles of Paris. She was simply brilliant, her wit sparkling, and she set a marvellous example for me to follow. However, I did not really feel at ease. I did not say much, and the few things I said seemed to make the wrong impression. The two gentlemen looked at each other with lifted eyebrows and my future fiancé became rather quiet. He looked at me with big eyes and it was obvious that his mind was racing. It seemed to me that he regretted his enthusiastic outburst when he first saw me.

However, a few glasses of champagne must have enlivened his imagination because soon he did not seem to care about my rather sober replies and he laughed at everything I said. He became more insistent, and I became a little bit more pliable. His good looks impressed me and it was obvious that he was a man of means and standing in Paris society. His hands took all sorts of liberties and I did not dare to push them away because I assumed that it was a form of good manners and I hated to act against the rules of good Paris society.

I thought about the splendid advice of the good abbot which proved to me that violation of the rules of society was much against God's intentions. I also believed that I should let things go as they were, because Uncle Bernard and his niece were sitting on the sofa in the other room and the liberties uncle and niece were taking with each other exceeded everything I had ever witnessed in Volno. Anyhow, I resisted the bold advances of Uncle Bernard's colleague so gently that he assumed he would have no trouble whatsoever in becoming a little bit more serious. He invited me to sit down upon the bed opposite the sofa on which we were seated. 'Oh, I would be delighted, dear sir,' I answered innocently. 'I am quite sure we will be far more comfortable because I am afraid that your present position on my lap must be terribly tiresome for you.'

You see, he had sat himself squarely upon my lap. Without further ado he lifted me off the sofa and carried me toward the bed. I saw that Mrs Bois-Laurier and her uncle got up and left the room. I, too, wanted to get up and follow them, but the passionate gentleman with whom I had been left alone seemed to have different ideas. He told me in no uncertain terms that he was deeply in love with me, that I drove him out of his mind, and that he intended to make me happy right on the spot. At the same time he grabbed my skirts and lifted them high above my waist. He held me with one hand and with the other he took his long and rock-hard member out of his trousers. He pushed his knee between my thighs; by pressing and squeezing he managed to part them. He patted my pussy and covered my face with slobbering kisses. He tried to wiggle his tongue between my lips and when I chanced to look down I saw the monstrous size of his prick. It reminded me of the holy water sprinkler which Father Dirrag used to chase the evil spirits out of the bodies of his penitents. It was huge and the red knob was throbbing.

Almost simultaneously I remembered what the abbot had said about the results of those actions. My innocent cooperation suddenly changed into a burning fury. I grabbed the bold rascal by his necktie and held him at arm's length so that he was incapable of fulfilling his attack. Without taking my eyes off the enemy, because I was afraid he would penetrate me with one mighty shove. I hollered as loud as I could for Mrs Bois-Laurier's assistance. Whether she had been in league with my so-called fiancé or not, she could hardly do anything else but come to my aid and scold the bold knave about his clumsy attack upon my honour.

Furious about the insult, I wanted to scratch the gentleman's eyes out. I told him in no uncertain terms what I thought about his miserable attitude and Uncle Bernard and his niece had the greatest trouble in restraining me and preventing me from attacking the man who had tried to make me pregnant. We struggled silently.

Finally, this silence was interrupted by loud laughter. The monster who had not ten minutes ago tried to violate me, was splitting his sides in one outburst of laughter after another. He had to sit down and wipe the tears from his face with a silken handkerchief. He put his tool, which now hung limply down, back in his trousers and said, 'I'll be damned. That little provincial bitch. Well, you must admit that I scared you, didn't I? Oh, oh, I can't believe it. They still make them that way in the villages. Such a silly goose. She doesn't have the slightest inkling what we were supposed to do here! Just imagine, my dear Bernard,' he continued, 'I put the young lady down upon the bed, I lift up her skirts, I show her my prick and what do you think happens? That stupid little goose thinks there is something wrong with that! She makes a noise as if she is going to be murdered, succeeds in getting the two of you out here and then goes into some kind of hideous spasm which would make you believe I did God-knows-what to her. I thought I would die laughing!'

And he started to laugh again. but suddenly he turned serious and said, 'But listen, Bois-Laurier, don't procure any of these idiots for me in the future. I am not a school teacher, and I have no desire to go through the trouble of telling every silly little goose from the provinces how to behave in my presence. You would do the little girl a favour if you taught her how she is supposed to act in a big city. Especially if she intends to meet other people of the rank and standing of Bois and me!'

I must admit that listening to this strange conversation made my head spin. I was totally flabbergasted, and I did not say another word. Bernard Bois and the gentleman disappeared without bothering to say good-bye and I lay half-conscious in the arms of Mrs Bois-Laurier who murmured something between her teeth to the extent that I, myself, was not entirely free of blame. We got into the coach that was waiting outside and drove back to our hotel.

The excitement had been too much for me. As soon as I was back in my room I broke down and burst out in tears. My chaste friend was very nervous and wanted to know exactly how I felt about the whole affair. She took extremely good care of me and did not leave my side for a moment. She tried to convince me that all men are curious and invent numerous ways to find out how far the girl they intend to marry is willing to go before they have exchanged the vows. It also gives them an excellent opportunity to discover how much the girl already knows about the joys of love. She closed her beautiful speech with the assurance that I had handled it correctly, though she hated to say that my vivaciousness might well have killed the goose that laid the golden eggs.

I answered furiously that I was no longer a little child, that I was very well aware what that miserable bastard would have done to me if I had given him the chance and, I added rather rudely, not any amount of money in the world was large enough to pay for having my body used that way. And in my excitement I told her what I had seen between Miss Eradice and Father Dirrag, and about the lesson which Madame Catherine and the abbot had given me.

To make a long story short, the clever Bois-Laurier managed to get the entire story out of me, and once she knew everything, her attitude toward me changed magically. She had noticed that I was rather unfamiliar with the customs and morals of the world and she was therefore very surprised about my knowledge of moral philosophy, religion and metaphysics.

Mrs Bois-Laurier was a very good-natured soul. She

embraced me, full of love, and exclaimed, 'Oh, how happy I am to get to know a girl like you. You have just taken away the veil from my mind, and in a flash I realize the mystery which was the cause of my unhappy life. I cannot help but constantly think about my former profession and I know that I will never be able to rest. Who, more than I, is afraid of the punishments of hell with which we are constantly threatened? And you, my dearest angel, have proved to me beyond a shadow of a doubt that my so-called crimes were involuntary. The beginning of my life was an incredible mixture of cruelties and, though it takes me all the courage I can muster, I will repay confidence with confidence and your wisdom with my experience.

'Therefore, dear Therese, I shall tell you the story of my life. It will teach you about the moods and tricks of men, and it is time for you to learn about them. They will contribute to your conviction that vice and virtue depend entirely upon temperament and education.'

And she began to tell me the story of her life.

THE STORY OF
MRS BOIS-LAURIER

You see before you, my dear Therese, a strange creature. I am neither a man nor a woman, neither a girl nor a widow, nor a wife. I have been a professional prostitute and yet, I am still a virgin. I am sure that you will think I am crazy, but please, be patient, and I will give you a full explanation. Capricious Nature has the path of delight which makes blooming women out of shy virgins blocked with an obstacle that cannot be overcome. The entrance is closed by a piece of skin that even the thinnest arrow Capid carries with him cannot penetrate. And you will be even more surprised to find out that nobody has ever succeeded in talking me into undergoing the simple operation which could cure my affliction. I am fully capable of enjoying the delights of love, and many girls who were born with a similar thick piece of skin in front of their pussy's entrance have shown me their operated parts and I have witnessed their pleasures with men. Evern since I was a little girl I knew that one day I was going to be a whore. And the mistake Nature had made seemed destined to ruin any profitable career. But, odd as it may sound, it has contributed greatly to my happiness.

I have already told you that my story will teach you a lot about the strange ways of men. I could talk to you about the many positions they have invented to penetrate a woman and to increase their carnal pleasures. But all these voluptuous positions have been described so completely by the famous Pietro Aretino, who lived in the sixteenth century, that there is not much left to say. What I am going to talk to you about is those flights of fancy, those curious services which many men desire from us, giving them the greatest delight and ecstasy, either because they have a preference for it or because they suffer from a physical defect. I'll come directly to the point.

I have never known my father or my mother. A woman named Lefort, who lived in Paris and who was reasonably well-to-do, raised me as her daughter. One day she took me aside, very secretively, and said, 'Dearest, you are not my daughter, and it is about time that I set the record straight and explained a few things to you. You were about four years old, and you must have lost your way to your home, when I found you wandering in the streets. I took you into my home and till today, out of love and

Christian charity, I have clothed and fed you. I have tried to find out who your parents were, but despite all my efforts I have never been able to discover them.

'You have obviously noticed that I am not very rich or important, but nevertheless I have spared neither money nor trouble ot give you a good education. But now you have to secure your own happiness. And, to be able to do this, I will make the following deal with you. You are very well-built, pretty and better developed than many a girl of your tender age. The president of the bank, my benefactor and neighbour, is in love with you. He has decided to keep you, provided you are willing to do his bidding. Well, Manon, he expects an answer today. What do you want me to tell him? I shall be honest with you. If you refuse his proposal, I shall be forced to throw you out of my house, today. You have to accept his offer and do whatever he desires from you, because if you don't, I'll no longer be able to feed and clothe you.'

This devastating news, together with the harsh conditions, filled me with a terrible fear. It was as if an icy hand had gripped my heart and tried to squeeze it out of my bosom. I burst out in tears, but my mother knew no mercy. I had to make an immediate decision. After I had been told what I might expect, and after I had been informed about the ways a man may know a woman, I promised to do whatever was desired from me. Mrs Lefort assured me that she would still care for me and love me as her own daughter, and she allowed me to keep calling her mother.

The next morning she gave me full instructions about my new profession, told me about my duties as a whore, and pressed upon me the importance of doing exactly what the president might desire of me. Then she made me take off all my clothes till I was completely naked;

she bathed me from top to toe, curled my hairs, brushed my pussy and washed it lavishly with lavender water. Then she handed me clothes which were prettier and cleaner than anything I had ever worn.

At four o'clock that afternoon we arrived at the home of the president. He was a tall, grey-haired, skinny man, whose tallow skin made his wrinkly face look yellow. His face almost disappeared behind a ridiculously high, white-powdered wig, which made his neck look scrawnier than it already was. This honorable personality invited mother and me to sit down, and he said in a very serious tone of voice to my mother, 'Well, well, well. So this is the little creature. She is very pretty. I have always told you that she had the potential to become well-built and beautiful. The money that she has cost me was spent well, I see. But are you sure that she is still a virgin? We'll have to check that at once, Mrs Lefort.'

My mother made me lie down backwards upon a couch in the room, she lifted my skirts and petticoats, and was about to spread my legs when the president barked at her, 'Come now, come now. These damned females have a positive mania of always showing the front! Now, let's turn her around!'

'Oh, I beg you a thousand pardons, my dear sir!' exclaimed my mother, cowardly wringing her hands. 'I understood that you wanted to see if she . . . hurry, Manon, get up! Put one knee on this chair and bend your body forward as far as you can!'

I did everything I was ordered to do. I was terribly humiliated, but I did not dare to refuse the woman who had treated me as her daughter, and I was terribly impressed by the importance of the president. My dear mother lifted my skirts again, the president came closer, bending over to look, while my mother spread the lips of my cunt apart. The honorable gentleman stuck one finger in and tried, without success, to penetrate. He said to my mother, 'Beautiful, beautiful. I am absolutely satisfied. There is no doubt in my mind, she is still a virgin. Now, I want her to stay in that position and I want you to give her beautiful buttocks some light slaps with your bare hands.'

The command was fulfilled, and a deep silence followed. My mother held my skirts with her left hand, and with the right hand she slapped my buttocks rhythmically, but lightly. I was very curious what the president would be doing and I turned my head slightly so that I could have a better look. There he was, sitting about two feet behind my buttocks, peering up my ass with a little looking glass, and his hand was busy shaking something dark and limp which was hanging between his legs. He never succeeded in getting it up, though he was trying very hard. His hand flew up and down, but the thing remained limp and ugly as ever.

My position was not too uncomfortable, and my mother's slapping had induced in me a rather pleasant glow. Nevertheless I was glad when, after about twenty minutes, the honorable gentleman got up off the floor, dragged himself on his spindly old legs toward his comfortable big leather chair. He handed my mother a purse and told her that it contained the one hundred gold pieces he had promised her. He honoured me with a kiss upon my cheek and he told me that he would personally see to it that I had everything my little heart desired, provided that I was as nice to him as I had been today, and he would let me know when he needed my services again.

When mother and I returned home I thought seriously about everything I had seen and my heard during those past twenty-four hours. My thoughts were like the ones you had, after you had witnessed the treatment Father Dirrag gave Miss Eradice. I started to remember a lot of the things that had been said and done since my childhood in the home of Mrs Lefort. And while I was still trying to make any sense out of the multitude of thoughts that stormed through my pain, my mother entered my room and rudely interrupted my daydreams.

'I now have nothing to hide from my my dearest Manon,' she said, embracing me, 'because you are now my accomplice in a profession which I have profitable conducted for over twenty years. Therefore listen carefully to what I have to tell you. Follow my advice and you will be able to get full compensation for what you have to suffer from the president. Ten years ago I took you into my home upon his express orders. During that time he has given me a modest yearly income which I have spent entirely for your education. Yes, I have even added some of my own money to his. He has promised me that he would give each of us a hundred gold pieces as soon as you are old enough for him to deflower you. He wanted to be the one to take your virginity. But the lecher has forgotten one thing. When you were old enough, he was too old. It is not our fault that he could not get that limp and wrinkled prick of his stiff enough to shove it up your cunt and take your maidenhead away. Since he could not do it, he has only given me one hundred gold pieces, because you are still a virgin and have not earned your share. It is too bad for you, but look at it this way: You can still sell it. Therefore, my dear daughter, I don't want you to worry. I will find you someone else, and you will earn more than the measly hundred gold pieces the old piker had promised for your defloration. You are young, you are pretty and, most important, you are not yet well-known. It will be a pleasure to spend the entire hundred gold pieces that were my share on a new and beautiful wardrobe for you. Let yourself be guided by me, and I assure you that together we will make more money than I used to make in former years when I had ten or twelve girls working for me.'

She had a lot more to tell me, but one thing was terribly clear to me, and that was that my dear mama had kept one hundred gold pieces all to herself. We made a pact. She would spend the hundred gold pieces on a new wardrobe, and I would repay her out of my first earnings with a modest twenty percent interest. After I had paid her off, we would share my earnings on a fifty-fifty basis, for which she would guide my career and continue to take care of me as if I were really her beloved daughter.

Mrs Lefort had an inexhaustible supply of good friends in Paris. In less than four weeks I was introduced to at least twenty of them and one after the other tried in vain to rob me of my virginity. Mrs Lefort was a very careful woman and she made it a habit to be paid in advance. She was, by now, convinced that nobody would ever succeed in tasting the joy of taking my maidenhead.

These twenty athletes were followed by more than six hundred others in the course of the following five years. Priests, officers, civil servants, lawyers and financiers made me take the most ridiculous positions, they contorted my body and theirs in the fruitless attempts to shove their pricks into my minute little orifice. Needless to say, none of them ever succeeded. Either the sacrifice was made at the entrance of my temple, squirting the jism into my pubic hairs, or the tool was bent and my virginity remained unharmed. Finally the story of my impenetrable cunt became too well-known and the police got interested in it. The commissioner decided to put a stop to all the fruitless attacks upon my innocence. Fortunately we were forewarned and Mrs Lefort decided that the time had come to put a little distance between us and the city of Paris in the interest of our safety. We moved away about thirty miles into the province.

Three months later the heat had cooled down, because a distant relative of Mrs Lefort, who happened to work in one of the police departments, had taken it upon himself to quiet down the upset feelings of his colleagues. We paid him thirteen gold pieces for his troubles, and returned to Paris, brimming with ideas for a new project.

My mother, who had for a long time insisted that I would undergo an operation, had realized that my affliction was a true gold mine. I did not need medical inspection, there was absolutely no fear of pregnancy, and I did not have to go to confession because the mortal sin of losing my virginity without the holy sacrament of marriage had never been committed. Unfortunately I, myself, found absolutely no enjoyment in my profession and I was forced to use the same means with which you, too, relieved yourself.

As I told you, we had come up with a few new plans, and as soon as our voluntary banishment was over we went back to Paris and moved into another home without, for one thing, bothering to notify the bank president of our return. We took a home in the Faubourg St. Germain.

The first acquaintance I made was with a certain baroness who had served the joys of famous men of the world together with her sister, a countess. She now graced the household of a rich English bachelor with her title and the sparse remnants of her former charm. He paid for them way out of proportion, but he was rich and happy at the mere idea of possessing a member of the nobility. Another Englishman, his friend, saw me and fell in love. We made an agreement. I confided in him and instead of being repulsive to him my confession delighted him. His first experience with a woman had been rather sickening to him, and he had sworn that he would never touch another one. Ever since, his hand had been his sole lover. However, he needed some additional excitement. His pleasure could only be served when I would stand in front of him with lifted skirts, while he jacked away furiously at his tool. But a maid, hired for the express purpose, had to cut little curls of public hair from my belly. Without this peculiar preparation the man was totally incapable of getting a hard-on and ten pairs of hands would not have been enough to get his prick stiff, let alone squeeze a single drop of jism out of his balls.

Minette, the third sister of the baronness, had a friend with a similar peculiarity. Minette was tall and rather skinny. Her face was ugly, her skin sallow and her temper was not always the most pleasant. But she had beautiful eyes, and her voice was fabulous. She tried to show off her passion and her intelligence but she actually possessed neither one. However, her voice could charm the dead. And it was this beautiful singing organ which had given her a bevy of admirers. The one she had at the time I knew her was only capable of getting his tool stiff when he heard the sound of her marvellous melodious voice. Only when she was singing was he able to shoot off his load.

One day the three of us had a big party. We sang and danced, made a lot of jokes and talked about all sorts of experiences, and also about the peculiarity of my cunt. We showed each other our charms, and mine was unanimously elected to be the most interesting. Minette's lover became excited, he pulled her toward the edge of the bed, shoved up her dress and stuck his prick up her pussy. He then ordered her to sing. After a few introductory warbles, Minette began a song in waltz tempo; her lover tore into her, shoved it up and pulled it back, the muscles of his face began to twitch as if indicating the rhythm and his buttocks pumped up and down to set the speed. I was lying on the same bed, looking at this ridiculous performance, laughing till the tears ran down my face. Everything went fine till Minette started to reach her climax, before her lover had reached his. She suddenly hit a sour note and fell out of rhythm. Then she shuddered and emitted a shrill shriek.

The effect upon her lover was devastating! 'Oh, you bitch!' exclaimed the music lover. 'That horrible note went through bone and marrow. And look what you did!' He was furious and pulled out his tool. The member which had been so proudly erect, which he had used like a conductor's baton, at the sound of the flat note had turned into a limp rag.

My girl friend was desperate and she tried everything in her power to bring her hero back to life. But the most tender kisses and the softest caresses were unable to bring about an erection. His tool remained limp and useless. 'Oh, my dearest friend,' Minette cried, exasperated, 'don't leave me. Only my love for you, and my fiery passion, caused my voice to break; please, don't leave me at this moment of my happiness. Manon, dearest Manon, help me! Show him your pussy! That will bring his powers back. It will surely make him regain his strength and save my life. I would die if he could not bring it to a finish. Please, Bibi,' she said to her lover, 'put her down upon the bed and make her take the same position as my sister, the countess. Manon's friendship for me guarantees that she will do it for you.'

During this entire ridiculous exchange I had been laughing. And really, has anyone ever seen somebody get fucked while she is singing? And then, can you imagine a man who fucks like a bull suddenly turning into a mouse because the woman he screws hits a sour note? Of course, I realized that the baroness' sister was not as deeply in love as she pretended to be, but I could understand her exasperation because she was being paid very handsomely for her odd services.

But I still did not know the role of the countess whose place I was supposed to take. I was not left in the dark very long. I had to turn over on my belly, and they put about three or four pillows under me. My arse stuck up high into the air. Then they bunched my skirts, petticoat and chemise under me so that I was absolutely naked from the waist down. Minette lay down upon her back and her head rested between my thighs. The hairs around my cunt framed her face like a wig: Bibi undressed his darling Minette and laid himself down on top of her, resting upon his hands. In this position her face, my cunt and my arse were all right in front of his nose. He licked and slurped without distinction. Now his tongue was between Minette's lips, then between my thighs, up my arsehole, into my pussy, and back between Minette's lips again. He even started to lick my buttocks. And meanwhile his member started to grow again and he began to pump away. Minette's hand guided his member back into her cunny and she began to swear and move her behind rapidly. I had turned my head around to get a good look and laughed till I ran out of breath. After they had laboured for what seemed like an hour, the two lovers finally reached their climax.

Not long after that I met a bishop who had the rather dangerous habit of roaring during the act of copulation like a maddened bull. Aside from the fact that it compromised some of his female visitors, it also endangered their eardrums. Whether it was to increase his satisfaction, or because of some organic disorder, as soon as His Eminence felt the tingling of his climax approach, he started to scream and roar, 'Aaah – eeek; aah – eeek!' The eeks and aahs were in direct proportion to the strength of his orgasm; the louder his roaring, the greater his ecstasy and satisfaction. The force of the fat prelate's ejaculation could always be measured by the loudness of his roaring shrieks. Were it not for the fact that His Eminence's manservant had been smart enough to cover the doors and walls of the bishop's mansion with thick, sound-dampening mattresses, the souls in Heaven would have been disturbed every time that holy man came.

I can go on almost indefinitely with descriptions of the strange things men do while they are in the act of coitus. With some it is the preliminaries, with others it is the additional little things they desire. Most of them wish a woman to be in a most peculiar position while they fuck them.

One day I was brought to the rear entrance of the home of one of this country's richest and most famous men. Every morning for the past fifty years he had received the visit of a girl he had never seen before. That particular morning it was my turn, and I had been fully instructed as to what to expect and how I was supposed to behave. The great, grey-haired lecher could only come in one particular way. He opened the back door personally, and, according to my instructions, I instantly dropped the clothes I was wearing and stood before him mothernaked. He sat down upon a big easy chair and with a serious face I turned around and offered him my backside for a good-morning kiss.

He planted a smacking kiss upon each one of my buttocks and cried out, 'Run, little girl, run!' fumbling in his trousers for his limp old tool. He shook it furiously at me and in the other hand he held a birch rod with which he threatened to beat my behind. I began to run and he followed me. We ran five or six times around the room, all the while he was jacking himself off and screaming at me, 'Run faster, you goddamned bitch, faster, I tell you!' Finally he sank exhausted and deeply satisfied into his easy chair; I dressed, he threw a few gold pieces at me and I left.

Another man put me mothernaked on top of a chair in the corner of his living room. I had to rub my pussy with a dildo while he was watching me from the other corner of the room. I liked that one, because it was one of my few clients who wanted me to come first. When he noticed that I started to pant his trousers would bulge, when I started to groan he would whip out his enormous dong with its big ruby-red knob, and at the moment I reached my climax, enormous squirts of jism would flow into his hand.

A third one – and this one was a doctor! – would be incapable of giving any sign of life unless a girl friend of mine and I had given him a hundred sharp blows with a whip. Then my friend would kneel in front of him, bare her breasts and he would start sucking her nipples. I would switch from the whip to a cane and hit him some more. Then my friend would begin to manipulate his balls and together we would jack off his slowly ripening tool. Finally we would be able to squeeze a little drop of jism out of it. This doctor maintained that flagellation would cure the worst forms of impotence and, moreover, that it would cure infertility. He had beaten several barren women, he claimed, and within the year they all had given birth to healthy boys.

The fourth one was a voluptuous courtier whose senses had been blunted by his youthful excesses. He, too, always invited me and my girl friend to his home. His bedroom walls and the ceiling were covered with mirrors. From his huge, red-velvet-covered bed — which stood in the middle of the room — one could see everything that was going on. 'You two darling girls are the most adorable little ladies I know,' he used to say, 'and I am terribly sorry that today I am not able to fuck you myself. Instead, if it is all right with you, I have instructed one of my manservants to have you. He is a very handsome and strong young man, and I am sure that he is willing to make both of you come. Yes, what do you expect, my beautiful little girls? One has to take his friends with all their little faults. One of my little faults happens to be that I'd rather do in my imagination what I see others do in reality. And besides, what could be more vulgar than a common fucking bout with a couple of ordinary peasants? It's too, too common. What would the world come to, if one of our standing should lay an ordinary, plump whore?'

After this honey-voiced introduction one of his servants would enter the room. All he would wear was an extremely short, flesh-coloured kilt. My girl friend was told to lie down upon the bed and the servant started to take off her clothes. Meanwhile I would take off my blouse and bare my breasts and shoulders. He only wanted to see my upper body naked. Everything had to be done with care and precision, and most of our movements were timed. The courtier would sit in a chair, watching the proceedings in the various mirrors from different angles. I would then walk over to him, open his fly and take his limp tool out of his trousers. Then he would wave me away with his hand, indicating that I had to sit down at the foot of the bed. Meanwhile my friend was supine and naked on the bed, the servant leaning over her, his marvellous prick stiff and proud as a rod. The happy man would look with expectant eyes toward his master, who would finally give the sign that the servant could proceed. The boy would thrust his weapon into my friend's body and remain motionless, waiting for further orders. His taut behind would be quivering.

'My dear little girl,' the cavalier would say to me, 'give yourself the trouble and walk over to the other side of the bed. And now, please, tickle those enormous balls of my trusted servant. Don't you see them, you stupid little female, those big things dangling between his thighs. Go on, tickle them!'

When I had followed his orders, the lordly gentleman would tell his servant to go at it. The boy would start to pump away at tremendous speed, and I would hold his balls, squeezing them lightly. The courtier looked in every mirror, his eyes soaking in every detail of the love game all around him. Finally he would succeed in getting his limp prick stiff and he would start jerking it like a maniac. When he knew that he was about to come, he'd shout at his servant, 'You can come now, my dear boy. Hurry up, squirt it into her!'

The servant would double his jolts and shove away with increased strength. Finally master and servant would simultaneously achieve ecstasy and squirt their juices in enormous spurts.

The things I just told you remind me of a rather funny adventure I had. It happened that same day and I tell it to you, because it should give you a good idea how firm the Capuchine monks cling to their chastity vows.

I had left the mansion of the cavalier and said goodbye to my girl friend. I walked around the corner and was just about to call for a coach, when an old friend and competitor of my mother stopped me on the street. Actually she was not so much a competitor as a colleague. Mrs Dupuis was also a procuress; but whereas my mother catered mainly to the well-to-do and off-beat circles of Parisian society, Mrs Dupuis' speciality was catering to the Roman Catholic clergy.

She exclaimed, 'Ah, my dear Mizzi. What a delight to see you. As you know, I am honoured by serving the clergy of Paris, and today it seems as if those dogs have made an agreement. They are all rutting at the same time. It's driving me crazy. I have been running all over town trying to find enough girls to satisfy their animal lusts. Now I am lookng for one who can help me serve three Capuchine monks who are waiting in the front room of my own home.

'Please, dearest Mizzi, help me out of my predicament. My feet are sore from running around and those men are getting hornier by the minute. Pretty soon they will run out of my home and rape the first woman they see. Please, Mizzi, come home with me, they are nice devils, and you will enjoy it.'

My protestations did not help. I told Dupuis that I was not a monk's chicken, that I knew the clergy well enough to know that they were not satisfied with using their imagination, that they did not enjoy a hand or a blow job, but that they demanded girls whose gates were wide open.

'Goddammit, are you crazy!' answered Dupuis. 'Do you care about their satisfaction? That is the silliest answer I have ever heard from a professional whore.

Listen, all they pay me for is to procure them a girl. What they want to do with her is their business. Here, look, they gave me six gold pieces. Three of them are for you if you will come along with me.'

Well, anyhow, she talked me into it. I did go along, more out of curiosity than because of the money. We got into a cab and drove to the home of Mrs Dupuis in the neighbourhood of Montmartre.

Immediately three Capuchine monks entered the room. It seemed that they were not used to seeing an appetizing young morsel like me, because they threw themselves upon me like three hungry dogs. I had just put one foot up on a chair to loosen my stocking. One, who had a huge red beard and a foul-smelling mouth, pressed his mouth upon mine and tried to stick his tongue between my lips. The second one grabbed at my tits with his plump, hot fingers. And the third lifted my skirts and pressed his nose against my buttocks, trying to worm his tongue inside my little opening.

Something prickly – I thought it was made out of horsehair – chafed between my legs. I grabbed it and pulled. What do you think I held in my hands! The beard of Father Hilarius. When he noticed that I had no intention of letting him go, the foul bastard bit me in the groin. I let go of his beard and screamed loudly. Fortunately this scream scared the horny monks for a second and they let go of me. I rushed to the other corner of the room and sat down upon the bed. But I barely had the chance to recuperate from my scare, when I found myself cornered by three huge, throbbing pricks. I called out, "Please, venerable Fathers, wait a moment. What we have in mind should be conducted with some dignity. I realize that I have not been hired for the role of the Holy Virgin, but, for God's sake, let's find out which one of the three I am supposed to take on first . . .'

'Me, me, me!' all three exclaimed simultaneously without giving me a chance to finish.

'Hold it, you milquetoasts,' said one of the three in a scornful voice. 'You dare to go ahead of your superior? What is happening to subordination?'

'Jesus Christ!' one of the two others exclaimed indignantly. 'What do you mean, subordination? There is no such thing in the whorehouse of Dupuis. Father Anselm has the same value here as Father Angelo.'

'You liar,' retorted the second of the two, hiting the venerable Father Anselm squarely between the eyes with his fist. This one, not a cripple either, jumped up and attacked Father Angelo. The two rolled across the floor, working each other over with fists and teeth. Their cowls were wrapped around their faces and necks, and their lower bodies were naked, the once enormous pricks flopping limply around. Dupuis tried to separate the two fighters but she succeeded only after she had emptied a bucket of cold water over their heads.

During the fight, Father Hilarius thought it better not to pay too much attention to unimportant details. I laughed so much that I was half-unconscious, reclining upon the bed. The good father made preparations to taste the oyster which his two comrades were fighting over. He was surprised by the resistance. He stopped and inspected my pussy closely. He opened the lips with his fingers and found to his surprise that the entrance was blocked. What now? He tried to penetrate again, but to no avail. He tried and tried and worked himself into such a state that he suddenly came and squirted his juices over the oyster which he could not swallow.

Suddenly everyone was very quiet. Father Hilarius had told the two fighting cocks about my physical disability and informed them that it was absolutely impossible to get a prick into that tiny little hole. They heaped scorn and abuse upon old Dupuis who just laughed. She was a very experienced woman and she knew how to rescue herself out of such a situation. She fetched several bottles of Burgundy which were soon emptied.

Meanwhile the tools of our venerable priests had resumed their firmness and the sacrifices to Bacchus were interrupted to bring sacrifices to Priapus. Even though I did not measure up to the qualifications of the clergy, they seemed to be very satisfied, because my breasts, my armpits, my thighs and my behind at one time or another were the altars of their sacrifices.

It did not take long ere a true mood of festivity had taken hold of all of us. Our guests took off their clothes and dressed up Mrs Dupuis and me in their cowls. They thought that I looked positively charming in this outfit. Dupuis, who was quite drunk, exclaimed loudly, 'Don't you people think that Mizzi is the most charming little monk you have ever seen in your life? Doesn't she have a pretty face?'

'Who gives a good goddamn about her face!' roared Father Angelo. 'Did you think that I paid my good money to see a pretty face! I came to your stinking whorehouse to fuck a cunt, not to see a pretty face. Why do you think I am holding my prick in my hand? To stick it in a cunt, that's why! And I swear before God Almighty that I won't go home till I have fucked somebody, even if it were the devil himself!'

'If it were the devil himself,'' repeated Dupuis, drunkenly staggering through the room till she stood in front of the venerable father. She bunched her skirts together, hoisted them up above her navel and exclaimed, 'Look at it, you miserable bastard! Do you see this venerable cunt? It is as good as two others. I am a perfect devil, so why don't you fuck me if you dare and I swear that you will have double your money's worth.'

And she grabbed Father Angelo by his beard, pulling him across her belly. The good father was not in the least shocked by the outburst of the old Dupuis. He was ready for a good battle and he put his lance in her before she had finished babbling. He shoved it into her with all his might and started to pump away.

Dupuis, who was sixty years old, had not found anybody in the past twenty-five years with enough guts to fuck her. All her pent-up emotions released themselves before the good father had had a chance to pump away more than six times. She started to thrash wildly on the bed where she was pinned firmly beneath Father Angelo. Her voice changed and she exclaimed, 'Oh, dear little Father, please fuck me hard. I am only a tiny fifteen-year-old virgin as you can see, and I need it so badly. Can you feel how I try to help you? Oh, oh, oh, I am so happy. Pump away, my dearest little cherub, you are giving me back my life. God will reward you, because you are performing a true labour of love.'

In between those terms of endearment, Mrs Dupuis kissed the monk wherever she could reach him and with her few remaining teeth stumps she tried to give him little love bites. The good father, who was loaded with wine, fumbled away as if he were a rank beginner. Finally the wine started to work upon Father Angelo, and Father Anselm and Father Hilarius who, with me, were interested onlookers in this battle of the century, noticed that the good Father Angelo had rapidly started losing ground. His movements were no longer regular and the force behind his shoves diminished rapidly.

'You goddamned bastard,' screamed the frustrated

Dupuis. 'I believe you're not even in! You miserable squirt, if you have the gall to . . .'

I will never know what Dupuis wanted to tell the brave Father Angelo because at that moment his stomach turned and he vomited all over Dupuis. When the old lady was covered by the stinking mass, her stomach turned over also, and she answered Father Angelo in a similar way, spewing all over him. The two of them swam around in their own filth. Father Angelo collapsed and fell heavily on top of Dupuis who tried with all her strength to free herself from his weight. Finally she succeeded in crawling out from under him. Dupuis suddenly turned vicious. She stomped and trampled upon Father Angelo, who did not even notice it, because he was peacefully snoring away. The two monks and I were laughing so hard that we did not have the strength to stop her. Finally we succeeded in calming her down and waking Father Angelo.

We washed them, dressed ourselves and at nightfall we all went our own way.

I do not wish to talk to you about those unnatural monsters who only find enjoyment with their own sex, whether they are active or passive. France, today, produces more of those monsters than Greece and Italy ever did. Of course you know the story of one of those afflicted who could only climax during his wedding night by summoning his manservant and ordering that wretch to do to him in the asshole what he, himself, was trying to do in his wife's cunt.

These faggots may make fun of our scorn for them, yes, they even defend their base tastes by saying that they don't act any different than their opponents, namely by following the dictates of their own natural feelings. These fiends say we are only looking for pleasure in the way we consider natural, and our opponents are trying to do exactly the same. So what is the difference, if our partners are willing? What business is it of you people who claim to be interested in women, and what business if any, is it of the women who scorn us? You must admit that we are not the masters of our own destinies and we cannot help having different tastes to you. We are accused of following a taste which is punishable by law. How ridiculous to outlaw a preference which has been given us by God. Why shouldn't we follow our desires since it is only for the satisfaction of partners who both want the same thing? What business is it of yours? Who are we harming? There is no such a thing as a punishable delight. And your argument that it is against Nature makes no sense at all, because it is Nature who gave us this particular taste to begin with. We are abused because we cannot procreate. What utter nonsense! Is there one person alive who gives in to his passions for the express purpose of creating a child?

In short these pederasts give thousands of reasons why they should be neither pitied nor scorned. But no matter what they say, I think they are monsters.

I have to tell you about a trick which I played upon one of them. My mother had made arrangements for one of those enemies of our sex to visit me. Even though I break wind often by Nature, I had prepared myself for his visit by eating enormous quantities of beans. I allowed the man to see me only because I did not want to disappoint my mother. Every time he visited us he spent two hours bending over my buttocks, sticking his finger up my hole and squeezing my buttocks, opening and closing them, and I knew he would have loved to stick something else up my arsehole. But, I had told him my opinion about him, which means, I abhorred him.

At nine o'clock that night he arrived. I had to lie down flat on my belly. He lifted my skirts and as usual he held a candle so that he could inspect me closely and gaze upon the object of his adoration. I had been waiting for this moment. He kneeled down and brought the candle and his face very close to my bumhole. His nose was almost in it. At that very moment I farted with all my strength, breaking a wind that I had been keeping back for almost three hours. It escaped its prison with a horrifying roar and blew out the candle. The pederast jumped back and the only thing I regret to this day is that I was not able to see his face in the darkness. He fumbled around for the candle which had slipped out of his hand, and by the time he had managed to light it, I had slipped out of the room and locked myself in my own little room upstairs. Neither begging nor threats could induce me to unlock my door, and finally the man who had received the biggest fart I ever let fly, left our home forever.

I thought that this was the most hilarious story I had ever heard and laughed so long that Bois-Laurier had to stop her story-telling. Two gentlemen of her acquaintance were announced and she told me that she was terribly sorry that I had only heard the seamy side of her life's story. She hoped that she would soon be able to tell me the good part so that I might learn how she had succeeded in escaping the sordid life into which the reprehensible Mrs Lefort had introduced her.

I must do Bois-Laurier the justice she deserves. Throughout my acquaintance with her she has never done anything to bring my good name in disrepute, except for that one occasion with her Uncle Bernard's colleague, even though she denied any knowledge of that man's intentions up to the very last moment we were together.

Four or six friends formed her entire circle of acquaintances, and I was the only woman she ever saw, because she said that she hated females. Whenever we were in company, our conversations were quite respectable but whenever we were together, just the two of us, we could have made a soldier blush. We had absolutely no secrets from one another and exchanged every little confidence we could think of. The gentlemen who visited her were all, without exception, respectable gentlemen of means. We usually played cards for very small amounts of money. The only man who was permitted to see her alone and in private was her so-called Uncle Bernard.

As I just mentioned, two gentlemen were announced. They entered, we sat and talked, played our game of cards and had supper together. Bois-Laurier was in an excellent and most charming mood; it is possible that she did not want to give me any opportunity to think about what had happened that morning, because she insisted that I would spend the night with her, after the gentlemen had taken their leave.

We said and did all sorts of things, but about that I may tell you some other time.

The day after that particular night, I met you, my dear count. It was to be my happiest day! Without you, without your advice, without your friendship and without the attraction we felt for each other the moment we saw one another, my life would have ended miserably, because I would have died without ever tasting the real joy of living.

It was a Friday, I remember it well. You were sitting in the amphitheatre close to the box in which Bois-Laurier and I had our seats at the Opera.

Our eyes met quite accidentally but we both seemed

to come under a strange spell, and we kept staring at each other. One of your friends who was supposed to take late supper with us after the Opera came to visit us in our box, and shortly after that you were talking to him. I was teased about my strange opinions on morals and theology, and you expressed curiosity. You seemed to be interested in finding out a little bit more about me and you seemed pleased when you were successful. The fact that you agreed with many of my opinions attracted my attention. So far, most people have raised their eyebrows in amused tolerance. I listened to you and I liked to look at you, finding a pleasure in these two simple acts which I had never experienced before. The pleasure was so strong that it gave me new inspiration, and it developed feelings in me of whose existence I had been totally unaware.

This is the way sympathy between two souls works. It is as if one thinks with the organs of the other. The moment I intended to ask Bois-Laurier to invite you to our supper, you made the same suggestion to your friend. We reached an agreement and when the Opera was over the four of us got into your cab and we drove away to your little palace. We played a game of cards in which you and I were partners, and we were so engrossed in each other that we had to pay dearly for the many mistakes we made. Then we had our late supper and Bois-Laurier and I had to leave. It was terribly difficult for me to say good-bye to you, and I was awfully glad when you asked my permission to continue our acquaintance-ship and if it was possible to meet me again soon. Your tone of voice convinced me that this was not mere idle talk and that you meant what you said.

When we drove away, Bois-Laurier was bursting with curiosity and she tried to find out, pretending to be totally disinterested, what we had been whispering during supper. I told her very simply that you had wanted to know what on earth brought me to Paris and, most of all, what kept me here.

I told her that your behaviour had been impeccable, that I trusted you, and that I had told you honestly what had happened to me. I furthermore told her that you seemed interested in me and had offered me your help and assistance. I repeated to her that you said that I had released certain feelings in you which you hoped to realize one day and prove by action that your passions were not mere words.

'You don't know men as well as I do,' answered Bois-Laurier curtly. 'Most of them are liars and are only looking for an opportunity to get a girl in trouble, after they have used her innocence. It is not that I believe the count to be such a person, on the contrary, he seems to be a man of honour.'

Bois-Laurier told me a lot of things, especially how to get to know the characters of the various types of men on the prowl. We went to bed together and we played with one another till we had reached several climaxes in each other's arms.

The next morning, when we woke up, Bois-Laurier said to me, 'Yesterday I told you the miserable part of my life; you have seen the bad side of it. But now I would like you to listen to me and hear the other side of the coin.

'For a long time I began to dislike the seamy life I had to lead, but I had absolutely no idea how to escape it. The money I earned always seemed to disappear somehow and the continual poverty kept me in bondage to the only profession I knew. Moreover, Mrs Lefort, who handled my affairs, was also the only woman who ever gave me advice, and since she had brought me up from when I was a four-year-old waif, she exerted an enormous influence upon me.

'Fortunately she became ill and died very soon thereafter. May God grant me forgiveness for the thought. Since no one doubted that I was her daughter, I inherited everything from her. Part of it turned out to be cash, there was a considerable amount of silverware and jewellery, plus, of course, the house, the furniture and sundry other articles that make up a well-stocked household. I kept whatever was necessary for a decent household and sold the remainder. It took me about a month to put my affairs in order and I bought a pension which gives me thirty-four hundred francs a year. I gave a thousand francs to the poor and departed for the city of Dyon where I intended to spend the rest of my days in a quiet atmosphere where nobody knew me.

'On the way to Dyon, near the village of Auxerre, I attracted a case of the pox. My face changed so much that nobody recognized me. This fact, plus the fact that the treatment and care in the province was horrible, induced me to return to Paris. I thought that if I stayed away from the areas where I had lived before my illness with Mrs Lefort and where I had plyed my trade, I could easily live in a neighbourhood where nobody would recognize me.

'I have been here since last year and only Bernard Bois knows about my past. He allows me to call myself his niece since I am now considered to be a lady of noble descent. You, Therese, are the only woman with whom I have ever exchanged any confidences and with whom I have ever been intimate.

'I am firmly convinced that your principles make it impossible for you to misuse the confidence of a friend, a confidence which you have won because of your outstanding character and your sense of justice.'

Mrs Bois-Laurier had finished her story. I assured her that she could count on my silence and I thanked her profusely for her confidence in me. She had proved to be a great friend, because it must have been difficult for her to overcome her natural reluctance to bare her sordid past. Yet, she had done it to me as a favour, so that I might draw a lesson from the mistakes she had made.

Meanwhile, it had become afternoon. Mrs Bois-Laurier and I were still paying one another those meaningless compliments which are demanded by polite society, when the maid entered and announced that you wanted to see me. My heart jumped for joy; I got up and ran toward you. We had very early dinner together and spent the rest of the day in each other's company.

Three weeks raced by, so to speak, and we did not leave each other's side. I did not notice at all that you used that time to convince yourself that I was worthy of you. My soul was engulfed in happiness and I could not think of anything but your nearness to me. I simply had no room for any other feeling than my passion for you, and though my greatest wish was to possess you for the rest of my life, it never occurred to me to devise a plan and assure myself of so much future happiness.

Meanwhile, I can now admit this, I was constantly worried about an apparent lack of enthusiasm whenever you talked to me, and a certain coolness which I could not properly define whenever we were together. If he really loves me, I told myself, he will hotly pursue me, just like all the others who keep assuring me that they feel nothing but the greatest passion for me.

Yes, I was very worried. I did not know then that

intelligent people are also intelligent in their love life and
that the fly-by-nights are flighty in everything they
undertake.

Finally, my dear count, after a whole month had passed,
you told me rather coolly that the situation in which you
had found me the first time we met, had rather upset you.
My face, my character and my absolute trust in you had
caused you to think of a way to keep me out of the mire
into which, you were convinced, I would shortly sink.
'Without a doubt,' you said, 'I must appear rather cold
to you, my dear Miss Therese. Especially since I am a man
who says that he loves you. I do not doubt that I love you,
but stronger than my love for you and my desire to possess
you, is my desire to make you happy.'

I wanted to interrupt you and thank you, but you did
not let me, and continued, 'There is no time for that, dear
girl. Please, be so kind and let me finish what I started
to say. My yearly income is twelve thousand francs.
Without making too much of a financial sacrifice, I am
able to assure you of two thousand yearly for the rest
of your life. I am a confirmed bachelor and determined
never to marry. I have decided to leave the city because
I am getting sick of the hypocrisy and idiocy that stares
me in the face wherever I go. I have a nice and
comfortable retreat about forty miles outside of Paris.
I intend to live there from now on, and I depart in four
days. Would you accompany me as a friend? Possibly
you might decide to live together with me as my mistress.
It entirely depends on whether you will find pleasure in
such a relationship. You can be sure that such a decision
can only have good results if you feel for yourself that
it will contribute to your happiness merely by wishing it.
It is proven that a person cannot feel the way he wants.
To become truly happy, a person must be able to secure

those delights which conform with his nature and his passions. He must, however, calculate the advantages and disadvantages these delights will bring him, not only to his own person, but also to those around him. It has been amply demonstrated that a person, because of his numerous needs and desires, can never achieve happiness without the help of a lot of other people. And he must take care, therefore, not to do anything which might harm the quest for happiness of those others. Whoever deviates from this rule will find that the happiness he chases keeps eluding him. This is my firm conviction, and the logical consequence is that true happiness is only possible for honest people. Men or women who cannot act with integrity will never be able to achieve happiness. The severity of the laws, their own pangs of conscience, their guilt feelings, the hatred and scorn of their fellow men, will be their constant companions.

'Take your time, my dear young lady, to think over what I have just told you. Find out for yourself, if you can become happy by making me happy. I will leave you now and come back tomorrow to hear your answer.'

Your words shook me deeply. I wanted nothing else but to make a man who thought like you the happiest man in the world. But at the same time I, too, saw the danger of making a grave mistake and I realized that your generosity would be able to prevent me from making that mistake. I loved you. But prejudices are extremely powerful and difficult to destroy. I was afraid to be known for all the world as a kept mistress, because it had not escaped my attention that a certain aura of disdain was drawn around those who were known as such. Moreover, I was terribly afraid to get with child, because both Madame Catherine and my dear mother had almost died in childbirth. Besides, I was used to providing my own climaxes, and I had been assured by everyone that they were as ecstatic as the embraces of a man. Therefore, I was unaware of the heat of my passion. I never had any carnal desire, because the mere thought of it was usually followed by immediate self-satisfaction.

There were two reasons left to decide in your favour. First, the possibility of a miserable end in the gutters of Paris and, second, the desire to make you happy and to achieve my own happiness by doing so. The first reason did not really disturb me, because its possibility seemed so remote. It was the second reason that caused me to make up my mind.

Oh, the impatience with which I awaited your return that next morning as soon as I had made up my mind! The next morning you arrived and I threw myself into your arms. 'Yes, oh, yes!' I cried out. 'I want to be yours and yours alone. Please, be considerate with the feelings of a young and innocent girl who adores you! Your feelings toward me assure me that you will never force me. You know my fears, my weaknesses and my habits. Allow time and your good advice to do their work. You know the human heart. You know the power that feeling has over the will. Please, I beg of you, use the opportunity to develop in me those properties which in your opinion are the best to contribute to your own happiness. Already I am your best friend . . .'

I remember that you interrupted me when I poured out my anguished heart. You promised never to go against my desires, and you also said that you would not force me to change my taste or to belittle my inclinations.

Everything was taken care of and the next day I informed Mrs Bois-Laurier of my happiness. She cried when we said our farewells and finally we departed to your estate upon the date you had decided to leave Paris forever.

Once arrived at that pleasant place, I had absolutely no time to think about the sudden change in my situation because my mind was constantly occupied with only one question: How to make you happy and give you satisfaction? Two months passed and you did not once insist upon my giving you certain pleasures, though you tried to awaken in me the desire to give it to you out of my own free will. I fulfilled all your wishes happily and voluntarily, only that one I was unable to give you, the one which you praised as the most ecstatic experience a couple could undergo. I could not possibly conceive that anything could be more pleasant than the delights I gave myself and which I offered to share with you. On the contrary, I shuddered at the mere sight of the monstrous arrow you showed me and was horrified at the thought that you would penetrate me with it. How on earth is it possible, I thought, that such a long, thick and stiff thing, with a head as knobby and big as that one, could get into a little opening into which I can barely stick my little finger? Besides, I was convinced I would die if I were to become a mother.

I begged you often to avoid this one dangerous cliff. 'Please, my dearest friend,' I would say, 'let me do it for you!'

I caressed, kissed, licked and rubbed your little Peter, as you called him. I moved him up and down and sideways, took the knob between my fingers and the shaft in a firm grip of my hand. My other hand would play with the bollocks hanging under your Peter and, whether you wanted or not, you would reach your climax and spill your divine seeds in my hand or upon my lips. The voluptuous delight would overwhelm you and you would quieten down again.

As soon as the carnal desires had disappeared, you would use my love for metaphysical theorizing and my habit of discussing moral problems to sway my opinion through the power of your word. One day you told me:

'Love for oneself determines all the actions of one's life. And with love for oneself I mean all those satisfactions we feel when we do something that gives us pleasure. I love you, to give an example, because I derive pleasure from loving you. What I have done for you is probably very pleasant and useful for you, but you don't owe me any gratitude. It is self-love which made me do the things for you I have done, because it gives me pleasure and satisfaction to do them. I am happy when I can contribute to your happiness. Therefore you can only make me completely happy when I know that your self-love is totally satisfied by doing so. Somebody gives alms to the poor. He may even go so far as to suffer certain inconveniences just to be able to give money to the poor. His actions are very useful, for the poor, as well as for society at large, because he is alleviating a certain burden of the community. Therefore his actions are considered very laudable. However, the almsgiver deserves no particular praise. He has given alms because his pity for the poor has caused him unpleasant feelings. And it was less unpleasant for him to give away his money than to look upon the plight of those who are poverty-stricken. It is possible that a certain amount of vanity contributed to his actions, because he liked to be seen by his fellow men as a philanthropist. But even in that case he was striving for a fulfillment of a certain desire. That fulfillment gave him satisfaction and the desire to attain that satisfaction is a form of self-love. All the actions in our life are caused by only two principles: To acquire more or less satisfaction, or to avoid more or less pain.'

At other times you would elaborate upon the lessons which I had received from my former father confessor, the abbot, proving to me the inanity of my prejudices. And finally you began to get tired of my eternal refusal. Then you had a brilliant idea. You ordered from Paris a collection of erotic paintings and books. Since I liked the books, and found as much enjoyment in viewing the pictures, you came up with two suggestions. You were finally on your way to success. 'Ah, you are reading, Miss Therese,' you said jokingly. 'Erotic books and pictures! Well, well, well! I am very glad to see that you are interested. I will secure for you the best available works in this field. But, with your permission, let's enter into an agreement. I will lend you for two weeks my entire collection of erotica. But you must promise me solemnly not to touch with your hands that spot which rightfully should be mine. You must completely and absolutely abstain from manual labour. There is absolutely no giving in, not for one single moment. We both must fulfill our part of the bargain. I have very good reasons for this wager. I leave it up to you. If you don't want to do it, then no more books, no more pictures.'

I did not hesitate at all and gladly promised abstinence for a mere two weeks.

'But,' you continued, 'that is not everything. Our mutual obligations should be of a similar value. It would be unreasonable to expect from you such a sacrifice just to view some pictures, or scan a stack of books. Let's make a wager which you are sure to win. I bet you my entire library and my complete collection of pictures against your virginity that you will be unable to stick it out for fourteen days as you promised.'

'Really, dear sir,' I retorted extremely irritated, 'you have unmitigated gall to think so lowly about my willpower and to overrate my passions so grossly.'

'Please, Miss Therese,' you exclaimed, 'please, no trial! I cannot argue with a woman who is losing her temper. Besides, I have the feeling that you have no idea what I am aiming at. Listen to me. Is it not true that your self-esteem is slightly damaged every time I make you a present, because you receive it from a man whom you are not satisfying the way you know you could! Well, my dearest Therese, you don't have to have that guilt feeling when you get the books and the pictures, because you will have earned them honestly.'

'My dear count,' I retorted haughtily, 'I realize that you are setting a trap for me, but I warn you that it is you who will be caught in it. I accept your bet and, what is more, I will take it upon myself to spend my days doing nothing else but viewing the pictures and reading the books. And I will start this morning.'

You ordered the entire library to be transferred to my rooms. I devoured, so to speak, in the first four days, a great number of books. I only looked up from them to view the paintings whose voluptuous compositions were portrayed with a beauty of coloration and forcefulness of expression which made my blood boil through my veins. On the fourth day a sort of ecstasy came over me after I had read for about an hour. I was still in bed and my bed curtains had been removed so that I had a full view of two particularly beautiful paintings. One was *The Festival of Priapus* and the other *The Love of Mars and Venus*. My imagination became overheated at the mere sight of those positions. I threw away my blankets and bedsheets. Without giving any thought to whether or not the doors to my apartments were locked. I began to imitate all the positions that were depicted in those two marvellous paintings. Every position I assumed gave me the sensation the painter had intended. A loving couple to the left of *The Festival of Priapus* excited me particularly, because the taste of the young woman coincided with my own. Mechanically my hand went to that spot where the hands of the young man were resting, and I was just about to stick my finger in my hole when I remembered the conditions of our bet. I stopped just in time.

I did not have the slightest inkling that you were a witness to my weakness, if you can call this delightful natural passion by that name. But, good God, what an idiot I was to resist the incredible delights of true ecstasy. But that is the power of a prejudice which had been pounded into my mind. It makes us blind, it is a tyrant. Other couples in this picture caused my admiration and some of them I felt downright sorry for.

Finally my gaze rested upon the second picture. What incredible voluptuous delight there was in the position of Venus. I stretched myself out, like her, comfortably on my bed. My thighs were opened slightly, my arms spread out wide. I admired the splendid position of the god Mars. The fire that sparkled in his eyes, and the power of his enormous member, made itself felt deep in my insides. My heart trembled. I thrashed around upon the bed, my buttocks moving lasciviously.

'What?' I exclaimed. 'The gods themselves are enjoying a happiness which I stupidly keep denying myself! Oh, lover, I cannot resist any longer. Count, please, come in, I am no longer afraid of your prick. You can stick it into your love, you can select any opening you want, only don't let me wait any longer! Everything is all right with me. I will enjoy your thrusts and to prove to you that you have won, here . . . look . . .!' And I shoved my finger deep into my hot pussy.

What a surprise. The happy moment. Suddenly you were there. More shining than Mars in the picture, more proud, more powerful! The light nightshirt you wore was thrown off in no time.

'You are too sensitive,' you said to me. 'I do not want to use the first opportunity. I have watched your struggle, I have seen everything. I do not wish to taste victory because of a trick. I only appear, dear Therese, because you have called me. Now I want to hear it again, from your own lips. Do you want me?'

'Oh, yes, I do!' I exclaimed. 'I am all yours. Shove it in and push as deeply as you can. Please, please, I beg of you! I am no longer afraid of your thick Peter!'

You sank into my arms and without hesitation I grabbed the lance which was quivering in front of my little hole, and I helped your enormous tool disappear into my cunt. You pushed it in deeply and your repeated shoving did not make me whimper once. I was completely engulfed by a delicious feeling and did not even think about pain.

Suddenly you said to me with a choking voice, 'I shall not use my full rights, Therese. You are too much afraid to become a mother. I will be considerate. But my climax is near. Clasp your hand around my prick the moment I pull it out of you, and help it with a few jerking movements . . . it is time, my love . . . I am dying with lust and pleasure . . .'

'Aah, so . . . am . . . I . . . I . . . am . . . dying . . . I . . . don't . . . feel . . . any . . . thing . . .!' I groaned, moaned and whimpered, all at the same time, shuddering in delight as I had never known before.

At the same time I grabbed your tool, squeezed it lightly with my hand which served as its new scabbard. In my hand you reached the peak of your ecstasy. Then we started all over again and our joys have now lasted for more than ten years. Always in the same manner, no children, no fear.

This, my dear benefactor, may have been what you wanted from me when you asked me to describe the story of my life as faithfully as I possibly could. If this manuscript is ever going to appear in print, a large number of blockheads and stupid prejudiced little souls will raise an outcry of disgust. They will criticize and scream about the metaphysical thoughts and they will pretend to be outraged at some of the descriptions. But they will also have missed the point of this book. The better for them, because I would not like to have it on my conscience to upset these stupid automatons. These are the people who act like pieces of machinery, who are used to thinking with the brains of others and who are petrified in their nightmares at the tiny fragments of original thought which once in a while surface in their minds. These people will be with us, I am afraid, throughout the ages, fighting a losing battle, but fighting nevertheless, because their stupidity, their prejudices and their ignorance prevent them from enjoying life as it could and should be enjoyed. The mere thought that others could find enjoyment out of life makes them vicious in their stupidity, and they will try to wreak their vengeance, and impose their moronic little wills.

Once more I will try to answer them. Everything I have written down is the result of my own experiences which I have tried to treat as intelligently as possible and, to my knowledge, as free from prejudice as possible.

Yes, you poor ignorant people. The concept of Mother Nature is a many-headed imaginary monster. Everything is the work of God. He gave us the need for food and drink, and also for the enjoyment of pleasures. Why, therefore should we blush and crawl away in shame, if we fulfill His intentions? Why shouldn't we contribute to the happiness of Mankind by serving many dishes, each of which is spiced with a variety of condiments and spices to serve and satisfy our many different tastes? Should I truly be afraid to displease God, or to incur the condemnation of certain people because I proclaim a truth which can only clarify and which could never do any harm? I repeat once more, you judges of so-called morality: We do not think the way we want. The soul has no will of its own. It merely reacts through the sensations of our senses which are caused by the matter surrounding us. Intelligence will explain this to us, but does not guide us. Self-love, the hope of experiencing pleasure or the desire to avoid misery are the mainsprings of our decisions. Our happiness depends upon the conditions of our organs, upon our education, and upon outside influences. If the human laws would be correct, they would be designed in such a manner that we could enjoy ourselves, by giving pleasure and by leading an honest life.

Yes, there is a God. We cannot help but love Him, because He is a being of infinite goodness and perfection. The intelligent human, the philosopher, should contribute to the well-being of society by His morally correct example.

There should be no religion. God is enough unto Himself. Knee-bending exercises and other contortions, the imaginations of other human beings, cannot possibly contribute one iota to His glory. Moral good and evil can only be an idea of Man, not of God.

The laws, enforced in great variety by every country, keep the communities together, and they should be obeyed. The ones who violate those laws, and who get caught, must be punished. The good example which is set by many so that those who are weaker can follow it, is as necessary as the punishment of those whose example tends to disrupt the happiness of society. If a king and his government want to be loved by their people, they should act only to the greater good of the people in their charge.

Angelica

Nothing about the grounds of the Abbey caused me the slightest unease, on the contrary, everything around me breathed abundance and gaiety, and as my relatives, whose companion I was, let me have my own way and never crossed me in any of my desires, you can imagine that I found this mode of living entirely to my liking.

Until my first communion the time passed easily and without the slightest care and though I was aware of the fact that the monks from a neighbouring Monastery were frequent visitors, I paid but little heed to the comedy that was daily enacted about me.

It is true they tried to keep me in ignorance of what was going on, from motives known to themselves, so that when I saw them caressing each other, I innocently attributed it to mere friendship.

As I often went into the garden with the sisters and their company, I became gradually attached to a young Bernardine monk who had always been kind and agreeable to me and to whom I owed my friendship out of pure gratitude.

In the course of time, changes took place which filled me with mingled wonder and fear, and which my cousin strove to allay. I passed the age of puberty and I noticed with pleasure the appearance of two little alabaster globes, ornaments of which all women are proud, but what interested me more was the fine down that began to show itself at a certain spot on my body and, wishing to know if my cousin had the same on hers, I managed to get a look one night when she was changing her undergarments, I saw then enough to convince me that mine was only a starter.

The next day after dinner we had company and I went with a party of them into the park. Dom Delabrise, the young Bernardine I have spoken of, after being absent for nearly six months, was with us and I confess I was very glad to see him again and he, too, seemed favorably impressed with my appearance.

A strange light glimmered in his eyes as he directed his glances towards me and while taking all kinds of sweet and tender liberties with my person, but without over-stepping the rules of propriety.

When I left him it was with a feeling that I cannot describe, love and regret mingled with one another, a feeling which only those who have themselves experienced it can understand.

I became pensive.

At this time an epidemic of smallpox appeared in the neighbourhood and I was one of those who first contracted this dread disease and this put for the time being, an end to my awakening love. For three long months I was confined to my bed, during which time I asked my cousin again and again if she thought that I would become pitted, for I was afraid of becoming ugly.

Dom Delabrise came three times to see me during my illness. The little attentions he showed me during this time contributed to increase the tender affection I began to feel for him. I was overjoyed one day when I heard him say that my beauty was not going to be marred in any way by the disease. Though I was only sixteen, my childhood had passed and my mind became wholly occupied with him whom I had learned to love.

Whenever I caught sight of him my whole body began to tremble as if it wanted to go to pieces. One day he came and asked me into the parlor and after kissing my hand, he told me that he had come expressly to see me, and as the sisters were busy that afternoon, he would be glad to entertain me alone, if I was willing. I told him that I was delighted and that I would be ready for him by two o'clock. He appeared punctually at the appointed time.

Kissing me tenderly and, as I thought, with more passion than usual, he took hold of my hands and began to pour into my willing ears many warm words of affection.

I was extremely green and answered only in monosyllables, although under the circumstances I was glad to play the listener.

Pretending to examine my collar, he touched my throat and I even scolded him for it. Judging from this that I was not inclined to be severe with him, he returned to the attack and kissed me most passionately, following up his advantage by running his hand up under my clothes.

I made some sort of resistance owing to that innate prudery that is found in every woman. As he did not give up the struggle, however, I let him go ahead and do as he pleased. The touching and tickling of his licentious fingers caused me the most peculiar sensations. Hearing someone coming, he made haste to escape. It proved to be my cousin.

'We must part,' he said. His eyes showed his exasperation and disappointment. I myself was vexed, for I was just experiencing a certain pleasure that I did not wish to cut short in such an abrupt manner.

It was surprising how easily one could approach without being noticed, especially in a *Paloir grille*, as this was. The room was partitioned off by a screen made of lattice work with two wings, which on being opened formed a little square closet, which was used to satisfy the demands of nature.

The rest of the day I was morose, thinking only of Dom Delabrise. The sisters noticed it and after supper, my maid asked me what was ailing me.

I replied: 'Oh, nothing.'

She then replied with a knowing look at the others: 'She is only growing and it is making her a little anxious.' I laughed with the rest, then got up and went to bed. I lost no time in falling asleep but awoke about midnight, after dreaming some of the strangest dreams.

I dreamt that my friend was at my side caressing me and that he had made me take hold of a certain thing, which I could not recall, having at that time no acquaintance with that part of man's anatomy. I awoke with an agreeable thrill and with my hand on my pussy, which I found to be slightly wet.

But that was not the first time this had happened to me; the difference was that I had not before taken much notice of it. I sighed instinctively, as any girl would under the circumstances. I also began to frig myself, confining my attentions to a little protuberance which was so sensitive as to put me beside myself with pleasure.

After playing with myself for a few moments I fainted from sheer pleasure and once again the sweet, dewy fluid put me under its balmy influence. Again I fell asleep, not to awake until my cousin returned from prayer.

Quite satisfied with my discovery, not a day passed that I did not repeat the operation, always thinking of my lover, whom I would have liked to have with me but he rarely came, as he was too much occupied with his studies.

A week passed during which I was left more alone than usual. My cousin absented herself more frequently, but being used to this I never inquired where she was or what she was doing. But wishing to finish a piece of work, she stayed with me one whole day and it did not displease me at all to have her company for she loved me a great deal, but at the same time it annoyed me, for I had to pretend a certain thing, to get a chance to enjoy with ease the little exercise I made my pussy undergo, and which I practiced in the toilet room.

She suspected something, however, and watched me, taking care though to slip away from her point of observation before I came out again. Having no idea of being watched, I satisfied my lustful desires and frigged my pussy until the desired thrill overcame me and then I returned to my work, and on entering, my couisn asked me: 'Angelica, where have you been?'

'Why, cousin, I have been to the toilet.'

'There is more than one thing that takes one to the toilet, I see,' my cousin said. 'I saw everything. Who in the name of mercy taught you to do it? It's nice, I must say.'

I was dumb with confusion, I threw myself on her neck and she did not repulse me but merely scolded me a little and left the room.

I suspected that she would go and inform the prior of what she had seen and I followed her and saw her enter his room. I quickly got up to the door and on her telling him about the occurrence, I heard them laugh, I then looked through the keyhole. Rosa was present, too. After indulging for a while in laughter, my cousin said to the other two:

'I believe you both would be tickled to death to have yours pulled.'

'Yes,' said the prior, 'I would for one; will you join us?'

A small vessel was placed over a flame and while Rosa

prepared an instrument about as long and thick as three of my fingers, the prior, who was a fine-looking fellow, sat in his easy chair and amused himself in tucking up his robe and rubbing his penis. Then he called my cousin and made her kneel in front of him and take his stiff tool in her mouth, on which, to my astonishment, she began to suck just as a babe sucks at his mother's breast. In the meantime Rosa had taken the vessel from the flame and poured its contents, which I now saw consisted of milk, into the instrument; this she fastened round her loins and, getting behind my cousin, shoved it up her cunt and began to work it back and forth. After a few thrusts, my sensual cousin closed her eyes, uttered a few a signs and then suddenly cried out: 'Let it shoot; let it come!'

Rosa pressed the bulb and the warm liquid was forced into her at the moment when the final spend or spasm overcame her.

At the same time I saw the prior stretch his legs and I was surprised to see some white fluid run down the side of my cousin's mouth. Rosa then took my cousin's place and she, too, received the same treatment.

When the erotic excitement gave way to calm and they all began to converse quietly together, I stole away to my room. I began to think over what I had seen and concluded that I had found the road to pleasure and that all I now lacked was acquaintances, and just at the moment that I thought of the warm milk that the sisters had used, my cousin entered.

'Well, Angelica, you have become more sensible, I hope.'

I did not answer but hung my head and appeared penitent, so she continued: 'Listen to me, my dear little friend, perhaps you do not know that it is a mortal sin to touch yourself in those parts; therefore you ought to confess and resolve never to do so again. Do not be angry, my dear child, because I tell you this. It may be a joke, but nevertheless, do your duty.'

'I am not angry,' I said, 'I will go to confession, but not to the Reverend Director.'

He was a hypocrite for whom I had acquired a singular aversion, not that he was overstrict, for he had been wild enough in his younger days and interfered very little with the sisters and their visitors. I abhorred him, however, so I shall not refer to him again in my story.

'Confessions are free,' was my cousin's response. 'Father Anselmo will be here on Monday and you may go to him.' I consented to this, though I felt very much like laughing in my cousin's face after what I had witnessed, but what would have been the use? We take things as we find them, you know. My worthy cousin feared that when I left the convent I might reproach her for not having first put me on my guard against the awakening of my sexual instinct.

I decided what course I would follow and I asked my cousin how I should best put the subject before the Reverend Father.

I awaited his arrival and began mortifying my flesh and only twice did I succumb to the temptation of employing my fingers to satisfy the burning lust of my slit, until the priest arrived.

On Monday, I presented myself before the sacred tribunal. I began as others do, saving the most interesting part of my confession until the last. I nearly put my confessor to sleep with a lot of unimportant trifles before I came to the real sin. His eyes began to shoot fire when I began to touch on the best part of my confessions:

'Ah. Oh! Oh . . . what is that I hear?'

'Yes, Father, I have sinned against my own person, both with my eyes and my hands.'

'And pray, against what part of your body have you sinned, my child?' This he asked in a soothing, fatherly voice.

'On that part that distinguishes the sexes!' I answered with downcast eyes.

He put several more questions of like nature to me and then having heard enough he said:

'Listen, child, I must hear the confessions of five sisters before dinner, I have not the time to hear the rest of your confession now but be in the parlour by one o'clock and we will talk the matter over.' He then gave me a light penance and sent me away.

At the appointed time I found him in the parlour; our conversation at the start was trivial enough. It was interesting enough for him, however, for he kept his eyes fixed on me most of the time. After a moment's silence he began:

'Now let us speak about those things; I mean about those terrible things of which you accused yourself this morning. Was it not immediately after your interview with the young monk that you began?'

'Yes, Father.'

'Not before that?'

'No, Father.'

'Did you not feel an itching round about that part?'

'Nothing of the kind, Father.'

'And you did not touch yourself until . . .'

'No, Father, I only rubbed it with my shirt.'

'Be candid, did you not feel pleased with the discovery you had made? Come now, speak out, don't be afraid of me. I am not a bad fellow,' he continued, taking me by the hand.

'To tell you frankly what I felt? Oh, I don't know how I could ever do it.'

'Promise me not to reveal anything and I will tell you things, child, that will set your mind at rest.'

I promised secrecy and he commenced thus:

'You have not done such terrible things as your little brain has imagined, for when nature makes known its wants, there is no wrong in resorting to those means to calm the violent feelings that overcome us poor mortals. But does it really give you pleasure to manipulate those parts?' he asked again, and eyeing me with fixed attention, he put a hand beneath his robe and I saw that he was fingering something.

The fact was that our conversation had excited the Reverend Father's sensuality.

He put his hand under my chin and kissed me and being too well pleased with his little discourse on ethics, I did not resist, besides he was a fine-looking man and still young, not over thirty at the most.

This little favour seemed to set him afire. He kissed me a second time and, undoing my neckband in spite of some resistance on my part, he gloated over the beauties hidden beneath, his eyes gleaming with passion.

'Oh, what a beautiful child you are! Why should I not be made as happy as that young Bernardino?' And coming over to where I was sitting, he grabbed one of my legs and with his knee against the other, he forced my legs apart, and then with his free hand he began to rub and finger my little pussy.

I bent forward, telling him all the time to stop, as somebody might come, but he pleaded with me so earnestly that I finally consented to let him have his way.

After feasting his eyes and fingers, he praised me most lavishly and then taking my hand, he placed it under his surplice. I withdrew hastily, thinking I had touched some venomous reptile.

'What ails thee child?' he asked. 'Don't be afraid, come now, I want you to get acquainted with it, touch it, finger it, that's the way, my little sweetheart.'

'And what is this thing, anyhow, Father Anselmo?' I asked as I began to handle it. 'My, how hard and warm it is!'

He now took it out and showed it to me and my surprise was great to see the difference between him and me. The instrument that I now held in my hand appeared to be about a foot long and as thick as my wrist, below I noticed a wrinkled sack hanging, which seemed to contain two objects that might have been taken for large eggs, for all I knew. I noticed also that it was surrounded by a bunch of light brown hair, which made it look like a white and red post sticking out of the tuft of moss.

He held my arm, begging me to have compassion on him and directed the movements of my hand as as he was of a strong and healthy constitution and easily wrought up to the spending point, he asked me to stop and then made me stretch myself at full length on the carpet. I made no resistance whatever. He admired my naked charms for a moment or two and then, with his right arm, he raised my posteriors. He fondled the fleecy covering of my pussy and then, rubbing a licentious finger along the lips, back and forth, he tried to sound the depths.

I begged of him to stop, for it hurt me very much. He would not listen and softly forced his finger in and then worked it in such a manner that procured me more pleasure than I had ever before experienced, and seeing from the way that I was beginning to heave and sigh that I was about to discharge, he gave me a voluptuous kiss and I lost consciousness in his arms. When I came to again, he was caressing me, fondly congratulating me on the sensuality of my nature.

So it was my turn to amuse myself at his expense. I became familiar with his prick, as he told me to name it. He lay down on the altar, still bearing the traces of my sacrifice to Venus, while I sat down on a stool, placing myself in such a manner that the reverend gentleman could reach my grotto of pleasure with his lips, then I raised his staff and how he enjoyed it. How pleased he was when I began fingering and caressing his proud tool; he cried out with pleasure.

'Oh, you dear little sweetheart, kiss me, rub harder, press tighter. I'm coming, I'm coming!' And, drawing himself up, he finally collapsed in a spasm and sank on the floor.

I felt something warm filling my hand and, looking, I saw for the first time that matter from which we spring.

'Well, now, you see the shape you have put me in!'

He only laughed and began to dry me with his handkerchief. To satisfy my curiosity, I plied him with questions which he willingly answered, one and all. I started as follows:

'I assure you, my Father, that I was very anxious to know how men were formed and I would have found out long ago if my cousin had not come in on us, when myself and Dom Delabrise were together, for he would not have failed to have spread his merchandise out before me.'

For all that I knew, the difference between one sex and the other was that one procures great pleasure from the other when they have connection. Still I did not know as much as I would like to know about it.

'Look here, child, here is a specimen that would soon enlighten you on that score and, although you are new at the business, if we were in a more convenient place, I would give you what you are looking for.'

'I understand, Father, but I am afraid your attempts on me would be in vain, for I cannot believe that my small thing could accommodate such a dagger as yours. You would split me in two.'

'It is true I would most likely hurt you at the start, but having it once lodged up to the hilt, you would experience a pleasure far superior to any that you have as yet enjoyed.'

'That means that the part of man is made especially to have connection with ours?'

'Without a doubt, the great author of Nature has created man and woman of different sexual attributes to that very end.'

'But what else besides pleasure results from this union of our parts!'

'Beings like ourselves.'

'Good, so that is the history of the human fabric. That white juice that I saw coming out of your thing, there, I suppose, is the essence which produces this effect?'

'Yes, partly, for it takes a woman's seed, too, to complete the work. These two semen coming together produce the foetus, which in time develops, takes life and becomes a baby.'

'I would like very much to have some fun with a man but I would not like to have it go so far as that. I would not like to have a baby, they say it hurts dreadfully.'

'Depend upon me, I can manage that part of it, for should I ever meet you in some convenient place, you will have nothing to fear. Now, for a little advice; if any one has connection with you, exact a promise that he shall pull his prick out of your cunt when he is about to finish, so that the discharge will fall outside on your belly, and in this way you are certain to avoid babies. But it is not the pain alone that you should consider about bringing babies into the world, it is also the law which brands you as an outcast when you have the misfortune to become a mother.

'I maintain, however, that you are entitled to all the joys of concupiscence you can get, provided, of course, that you have some regard for appearances. Those men or women who are forced by circumstances to remain single, whether it be on account of lack of means or cupidity of their parents, who have forced them to adopt a life that condemns them to a state of celibacy, those people, I say, should not be obliged to forego the pleasures of sexual intercourse. Nature has supplied them with organs and Nature intends that they shall use them. So let me say, once more, one may amuse himself or herself under any conditions, taking only the precautions not to run afoul of our iniquitous laws, which seem to have been formed only to tyrannize the weak.'

'I will bear in mind what you have told me, but see, it is almost three o'clock. I am afraid my cousin will soon be looking for me.'

'Don't be uneasy about your cousin, she is very busy and will not bother her head about you for some time yet.'

'Why, what in the world is she doing?'

'If you wish to know what she and the prioress are doing this very minute in the sacristy, go listen at the door, then come back and tell me what you hear.'

'I have an inkling of what may be going on in there.'

'You have? How is that?'

'A few days ago I saw my cousin and Rosa amusing themselves with some strange instruments.'

'I think I know what you mean. It is what is called a

dildo. Each one has a good friend who caresses her with it and I am sure you will be shortly initiated into the joys of dildo fucking. Now, do as I told you and if you cannot see anything, you will doubtless hear something.'

I went off and, after finding what Father Anselmo had insinuated I would find, I returned and reported to him.

'You spoke the truth, Father Anselmo, I recognized the voice of the parish priest, and as near as I could judge, he was serving my cousin as you said − of this I was convinced from the way in which the Mother Superior addressed Dom Lamotte, the parish priest.

' "You will fuck me once more, dear Father. The others have had their fill and I can stand a good deal more than they can, so give it to me once more."

'Then everything became quiet for several minutes, only interrupted by an occasional kiss. Then I thought I heard the squeaking of the sofa.'

'You see, Angelica, I was right, but what ails you now? Did it give you a funny feeling? Your cousin won't be back for some time yet, let us make use of the opportunity. Take up your dress and let me see that lovely cunt; how brown you are getting there. Now turn around. Oh, what a beautiful arse, so white and round; you are sighing! Now hold your legs apart and we will see if we cannot make this mossy love fountain spout forth again.'

'Oh, oh, dear Father . . . I cannot . . . oh, I cannot speak . . .'

'Are you enjoying it, sweetheart?'

'Yes, and I am going to repay you if I can. But first let me look at it, your prick, I mean; is that the right word? It looks like a nutcracker about the head. That makes you laugh, and what are these two things in the pouch? What a lot of hair there is around here?'

'Those, my dear, are the testicles, or as you should call

them, the 'balls.' All males, men as well as animals, have them and those that have them not are not able to fuck. Hold on, Angelica, I am coming. Here it comes, kiss me, child.'

'Did I do it right?'

'Yes, you bet you did! Let us get up.'

'Now tell me about the dildos. Why do they put milk in them? That puzzles me.'

'I will tell you why. You see, women are not provided with willing servants as the nuns here are, who lack nothing in this respect as you have just seen. They are compelled to find solace with one another, and the hot milk which they inject produces almost the same effect as if they had connected with a man. Still there is a big difference for, after all, a dildo is but a lifeless instrument and one can never give as much pleasure as a prick.'

'Now let me look at it again. My, what a queer-looking object it is, now what causes it to undergo such a change as that? Don't laugh, what in the world becomes of all the stiffness? And the head of it that looked so red and inflamed, what made it come down in such a short time? And it has not the same colour at all; and the skin that nearly covers it now; I did not notice it at all before.'

'This change that it seems surprises you so much is in reality its natural condition. If it were always in that state in which you saw it at first, it would be very inconvenient. Only occasionally it takes that form. The sight of a woman or even our imagination will cause it to stiffen and stand up proudly, which goes to prove that the man was made for the woman and the woman for the man.'

'That is strange. See, it is getting hard!'

'It would have to be a stick or a stone if a hand like yours would not bring it to life again, but that is enough, it exhausts a person when carried to excess, and you ought to restrain yourself and only do it when your desires overpower you, for as you are not fully developed yet, excess would do great harm. Do not mention anything of what I have told you or of what has taken place. I will come to see you again and then I will bring you a dildo proportionate to your age, so that you can amuse yourself. Good-bye, sweetheart.'

I will ask the reader not to criticize the poor Franciscan monk too severely; I, for my part, bore him no ill will for having taken advantage of my youth and inexperience.

After the Franciscan left me, I retired to my room, very well satisfied indeed, my cousin putting in her appearance shortly after, her face flushed and seemingly suffered from the heat. 'When did Father Anselmo leave?' she asked.

'At two o'clock, my cousin.'

'And what did he say to you when you confessed your little pranks?'

'He forbid me to do it again.'

'Very good, but you do not look as if you had followed his advice.'

'Why, dear cousin?'

'Because your eyes pronounce the contrary.'

I smiled and threw myself on her neck.

'Don't hang on me so, my little friend, for I am terribly warm. Let us work together until supper time,' she said, giving me a motherly kiss.

Then while we were working she regaled me with an account of the beauties of a religious life, although I had already told her that I would embrace it, if for no other reasson than to be always near her. I repeated my promise, taking a most solemn oath to that effect. From that time the most cordial relations have existed between us to the present time. Mamma, who came to see me quite often, was well pleased with my final resolutions and announced it with greater amiability than usual.

The following day at eleven o'clock in the morning, Dom de la Platier and Panza came to the Abbey. One was the lover of Rosa and the other was Agatha's. As I wished to see them together and judging that they would make use of the same room in which I had seen my cousin, I scouted around a little and found an old entrance to an unused hallway, which ran along the back part of the building. I examined the wall and discovered that it was broken in a place where I had only to pull aside a piece of tapestry to gain a full view of the room.

My cousin had told me that she would spend the afternoon with the Abbess, so I went and took my place at the peephole in the wall. I was waiting some time, when finally they arrived. Agatha locked the door behind them and put the key into her pocket. Veils and skirts were soon cast aside, instruments of war were displayed and seemed in good condition. All four threw themselves on the bed where, after an exchange of a few sweet phrases, they placed themselves in position for the sacrifice.

I had a full view of the posteriors of the reverend gentlemen, which were going like steam engines, while my ears caught the sounds of disjointed words and exclamations, such as: 'Fuck . . . ah . . . deeper . . . quicker. I could d-i-e . . . fuck; keep on, you dear f-u-c-k-e-r.'

But then there is a limit to everything and this sport of pleasure is no exception. Dom Panza was the first to roll off, exposing as he did so the cunt of the slender blonde, and if cunts shed tears, hers certainly was doing so. Flowing down the crack of her splendid arse, they formed a pool on the towel they had so thoughtfully placed there. The other two came in a close second.

They were still in the act of drying their parts when my cousin, who I thought was still with the Abbess, happened to pass close by the corridor in which I was stationed, caught sight of me and, coming up softly, beckoned me to follow her. My confusion was too great to describe. I ran hurriedly away and was the first to reach our room.

'That is very nice, I must say, to play the spy like that!' she said in a low tone. 'If the sisters knew that you had spied on them, they would never forgive you.'

I must have looked very downcast, for my cousin came and threw her arms about me and, bursting into laughter, she began to reassure me. 'Come now, Angelica, don't be afraid,' she said. 'Truly, I would not have them know it for anything in the world, but tell me how you came to peep at them?'

Mustering a little courage, I answered: 'I was on my way to the park and while passing through the corridor, I heard queer noises to my right, so I looked to see what it was. I hadn't been there more than a second when you came along.'

She eyed me steadily for a moment and began: 'What you have seen prompts me to tell you sooner than I had wanted to of many things that are being done here. Of course, you have been kept in ignorance until now, but I must exact a promise from you never to divulge either what you have just seen or what I am going to tell you now. Since you have made up your mind to stay with us, I will reveal all to you this evening, keeping nothing back.'

'Oh, cousin,' I replied, 'I shall be very discreet; depend upon it.'

Then we embraced each other and went to the

apartments of the Abbess. We had supper with her, after which we returned to our apartments and as soon as we were in bed, we resumed the conversation. My cousin — Felicity was her name — began thus:

'Because I wished to have you always with me, I induced you to embrace the life of a nun, but I swear that if I had been unhappy, I would have warned you not to take this step. But as it is, I consider myself happier here than I could ever hope to be in the world.

'Here we have all the enjoyment of life without its inconveniences. Women were made as companions to men, and this maxim is practiced, if not openly preached, in this convent, and you have seen how pleasant it is to have one's arms and legs twined about a man capable of satisfying one's wants, you will learn more of this later.

'I noticed with pleasure how you were growing and, better still, how sensible a mind you had. Onion peddlers know each other even in the dark, so you need not be surprised when I tell you that your little prank with Dom Delabrise did not escape my attention when I surprised you in the parlour together. One look was enough; I knew as well as if you had told me what had taken place. I am delighted that you have taken a liking to him and, far from putting any obstruction in the way of your lovemaking, I will do all I can to bring you two together as often as possible.'

'Oh, how much I am obliged to you, dear Felicity. Yes, I do love him. I conceived an affection for him even before I knew why, but really I feel a tenderness towards him that I cannot explain. I might say that I love him through some kind of present that he can contribute to my happiness and I am never happy when I am not in his company. The day you surprised us in the parlour was a cruel intrusion for me, for I enjoyed myself with him.'

'Had you already accomplished the act? You know what I mean!'

'No, but his hands were feeling all over and the sweet kisses he was showering on me gave me so much enjoyment that I have ever since had a longing for his company.'

'No doubt he did not fail to show you what he had?'

'No. I am sorry to say, you came in on us too soon but I have been doubly repaid by the splendid view I had of Dom Panza and Dom de la Platierre.'

'And what did you think of their tools and the manner in which they used them.'

'I saw that they were strangely made and of enormous size and capabilities, and I wondered greatly how such big things could disappear in the bushy depths between the sisters' outstretched legs and also at the every quickening in-and-out motion and movements of the sisters' arses. All this seemed to give general contentment, both to the givers and the takers.'

'And what did you do all this time, Angelica?'

'I was all on fire and I wished to be treated in the same manner, and this being out of the question I decided that if this could not be a duet than I must content myself with a solo.'

'Never mind the solos, some day you will play duets and quartets, too, only do not rush things, just keep cool and wait. Dom Delabrise suits you. He is a handsome young fellow, I congratulate you on the choice, but listen to my advice.

'We all make mistakes and you made one when you let him take so many liberties with you on so short an acquaintance. You should never throw yourself at a man's feet like that, nor let him guess that you are as passionate or even more so than himself.

'It is only after a great deal of attention and perseverance on their part and after giving an undeniable proof of their regard by an assiduous courtship that we should accord them a small favour. This makes them more ardent lovers, more devout worshippers at the shrine of our charms. It is in this way that we must lead them on. Now, take me, for instance: I have a good friend in the parish priest, you must have seen us often together.

'Now, do you imagine that I abandoned myself to him all at once? I should say not. Many a time I have heard him plead and sigh, many a time I have seen him on his knees begging me to have pity on him, assuring me with heartrending sighs that he could never live through his martyrdom, so whatever favours he now receives, he paid for dearly.

'And when your friend comes, I promise he shall be yours on condition that you keep him in suspense for quite awhile before you grant him the last favour.'

'I understand now, my dear Felicity, I have been so easy.'

'No doubt you have.'

'You can leave it to me. I will bear in mind what you have told me, only I think I am taking a great risk. I might lose him because . . .'

'Because your sensuous nature torments you, that's it. We all have passed through the same trying process but rather than lay down my arms, I'd sooner use a candle. It is always that way with people who do not wish to listen to good advice and let their passions get the best of them, and it usually ends disastrously. I do not feel like saying any more tonight. Let us sleep now; more on the subject some other time.'

Before going to sleep, I reflected on what my relative had told me. I was overjoyed at the thought that from now on I could see Dom Delabrise without trouble, and I formed plans how to act when in his company. My little intrigue with Father Anselmo had taught me many things and he, too, would not meet with the same complaisance on my part as heretofore.

The following day my cousin completed her revelations as to the amorous life the sisters were living and I renewed my promise to take the veil as soon as I was of proper age.

After dinner I took my work and went to the Mother Superior. She received me in a cold, reserved manner. I responded in the same way. I also called on several of the sisters, who received me with more cordiality. But the one who pleased me the most was Suzanne, whose acquaintance the reader will make in the course of my history.

What I longed for, for a long time, finally arrived in the shape of a letter from Dom Delabrise and it tended to rouse my drooping spirits more than anything else that could have happened; he wrote:

Dear Angelica:

I was in hopes of seeing you yesterday but an unhappy chance deprived me of that pleasure. I hope, however, soon to be able to tell you with word of mouth what my pen cannot explain in a proper manner.

If ever a man fully appreciated his good fortune it is myself, your humble servant, I assure you, entrance into the convent was the beginning; and you were at that age when you couldn't understand what love is. I was drawn to you by some invisible force. I thank my good fortune that I enjoy seeing the little flower which I might say I planted with my own hands blossoming out into a beautiful rose, which I flatter myself is for me to pluck.

Dear Angelica, twenty times a day I leave my most serious occupation just to let my mind dwell on thoughts of you. I can hardly wait for the time when I can tell you how worthy you are of my deep and sincere love; it is my hope that our superiors will not again break up our sweet tête-à-tête.

With a love that cannot be written, I have the honour to be,

Your most humble servant,

DOM DELABRISE

Showing this letter to my cousin, she made me promise to treat him with more reserve than before, so I answered him in the manner indicated below:

Dear Sir:

Your letter is full of kind expressions, but kindliness on your part is not new to me, so I assure you of my heartfelt gratitude.

I invite you to come whenever you wish, you will always be well received, provided you keep yourself well in check and do not become too enterprising.

My cousin, who is a very farsighted person, reproached me severely and you know I had reason to reproach myself. You have lost my esteem but you may regain it again by never placing me in the same embarrassing position, which would force me to withdraw it.

Yours truly,

ANGELICA

After dinner the same day, the parish priest, Dom Panza and Dom de la Notte, came into the Abbey. Their ladyloves joined them after dinner and I went to call on

Suzanne. I would have much preferred to spy on the three amorous couples, but it was expressly forbidden and what really prevented me spying was that they had chosen a room that was tightly closed.

At night my cousin had her confidential chat as usual. I started in:

'I have passed a long and tiresome afternoon, though Suzanne is a charming girl I was not at ease with her and consequently our conversation was uninteresting.'

'You know what I told you, Angelica, don't precipitate anything with the sisters, let them make advances first. None, besides the prioress, know that you are aware of our amours, and Suzanne is not yet one among us. She has been struggling against Dom Bigot for nearly a year and has not surrendered yet, but I think nevertheless she will soon come into our dovecote.'

'Did you not enjoy yourself very much this afternoon?'

'My admirer proved his love four times.'

'And the prioress?'

'Just as much, with this difference, that she has not got to adopt the precautions that we do; so there is nothing wanting in her enjoyment, which is therefore much greater.'

'Then she runs no risk of getting knocked up?'

'She has been going through this performance for ten years and nothing has happened to her yet. There are lots of sterile women and she is one of them. I am not fool enough to take any chances, and I advise you to look out for your own little affair. Now let us sleep, but where are your hands?'

My cousin was not mistaken, for during our conversation I had been rubbing and fingering myself until I brought on the crisis just when she ended her admonition.

'There on my breast.'

'Come now, don't do that too often, it is harmful.'

The prioress called on us the next day, bestowing upon me more than the usual attention and consideration.

'Now, Angelica,' she said, 'don't fib, why did you not say your devotion today?'

I reddened and looked helplessly at my cousin.

'Speak up, now, do not be afraid of me, I am one of the girls myself.' She gave me a kiss and I returned it warmly and allowed her to examine me very thoroughly.

'There is quite a lot of down sprouting on it already,' she said, addressing my cousin. 'It is beginning to darken this fluffy spot here, what do you think Felicity, is she not fit soon to be on the peg?'

In return I said many funny things; among others, I asked her why moss was growing on such funny things. She answered saying that all she knew about it was that it was natural for one's cunt to wear tresses.

We went for a walk and while passing a small cabinet in the park, I saw Suzanne with a Franciscan monk, who was looking very downcast. I made my thoughts known to my companions, who enlightened me on his history.

The next day the lovesick monk returned to the charge but in vain; he finally decided to let Agatha plead his cause for him. In the following I will endeavour to give part of the conversation that I overheard between Dom Bigot and Suzanne.

'How can you be so severe with me, Suzanne? Have compassion on me and reward my faithful love and grant me the favour you crave yourself.'

'It is of no use; it can never be. Why can we not love each other without . . . no. No . . . it cannot be, I tell you.'

'You torment me beyond all description, if you were

less beautiful, my suffering would be less; pray have pity on me. Why do you wish to avoid me? Can nothing that I say have any effect upon your obstinate will?'

'It cannot be. I repeat it, no. Be done with it.'

'Oh, Suzanne, by all that I hold dear in this world, I promise . . .'

'Come, come now, my fine gentleman, so that is what you wish, is it? Well, make your mind easy; no man yet got the best of a woman against her will. You are an ungrateful wretch. Now leave me; I never want to see you again.'

Our fair one tore herself from his grasp and seemed greatly exasperated.

Agatha, following a sign from Dom Bigot, appeared upon the scene to lend her assistance in overcoming the scruples of the fair nun. Addressing Suzanne, she said:

'How are you? What on earth ails you, you look so cross. Is it because Dom Bigot is leaving so soon?'

'Please don't mention his name in my presence again. I don't like him, and if you have come to talk about him, you will do me a favour to retire.'

'Calm yourself, dear friend, and try to bring back the cheerful smile that is becoming to you, yes, I can speak to you about him, and what is more, I want you to listen. If you had only seen him as he went out, he was not the same man anymore. He begged me with tears streaming down his face to set him right with you and I am confident that had I not promised to intercede with you in his behalf, he would be tempted to do something rash. Such love, Suzanne, deserves a better fate.'

'Actions speak louder than words with me, dear Agatha. When one loves, he conforms to the loved one's wishes. He knows what my thoughts are on certain things and he has promised me a hundred times never to give offence to them, and just as often he has failed to keep his word.'

'His conduct is a proof of the love he bears you. He has only had eyes and ears for you and no one else but you. Now if his love was not sincere, he would have tried to get even by making love to one of us. I give you credit for that but I think it would have done him a better service with you if he had been less attentive and had made you a little jealous by paying attention to one of us, but he is altogether too honest for that; he never even gave us a pleasant word or a smile. There was no one for him but Suzanne. I for my part think him a very handsome and attractive young man, and if I did not like you so much, I would set my cap at him.'

'And what does that signify; have you not one already?'

'Good. Good. I could just hug you for those words; your heart betrays you. You are being moved to pity; you love him, you cannot deny it. It was not today that I found this out. Now, why don't you accord him that supreme happiness?'

'Since you have discovered my secret, I will make a clean breast of it to you. I have confidence in you and will tell you all, keeping nothing back. I love Dom Bigot as well as he ever loved me and I am sure my pleasure would equal his own if I let him have his way. But the fate of poor Richardierre is still fresh in my memory and I dread to undergo the same terrible ordeal.

'When I pulled away so suddenly, it was through fear that I would succumb. I did violence to my own desires in doing so, I assure you. If I pretended to disdain his lance it was not because I feared to have it pierce me, but I kept on repeating all the time to myself: Dom Bigot is a young and vigorous man and as soon as a free passage is offered him, he will stretch and tear me unmercifully, and then he will lose all self-control and my poor body will be the sufferer. This is the reason why I do not give in.'

'Your fears are ill founded, my dear Suzanne. It is as much in his interest as yours that he should spare you, and he would therefore never think of causing you unnecessary pain. He is to return in three days; now tell me what I am going to tell him when he returns?'

'Oh, you are terrible; how you lead me on! He may come, however, he will never dare to make proposals, and you may be sure I will not make any advances.'

'Don't trouble yourself on that score, I will give him the necessary hint.'

'What is it you say? Please don't promise him success.'

'All right, let us go for a walk.'

La Richardierre, whom Suzanne referred to, was a young woman who had an affair with a rash devil-may-care fellow who knocked her up. Her worry and remorse were so great that she died before she gave birth to the fruit of her womb.

My cousin told me that Suzanne's affair was as well as settled and she would soon be initiated with all due formalities into the society. My curiosity being aroused, she promised to satisfy it in some other way, arranging it so that I might be a spectactor at the ceremony, taking care to place me where my presence would not be known to the priests or nuns.

After dinner, Dom Delabrise asked to see me in the parlour. I was a little embarrassed at the meeting but recovered myself. I answered his questions as easily as I could. For a while my answers kept him respectful, but soon his passion got the best of him and he became daring. I gave him to understand that if he did not behave I would leave the room.

'How coldly you treat me!' he said. 'My unfortunate absence has worked a great wrong, I see.'

'There is no coldness on my part,' I answered. 'I am delighted to see you, but remember what I told you in my letter.'

'Only too well for my peace of mind; I greatly fear someone has supplanted me in your affections.'

'You have a strange opinion of me, Dom Delabrise; I know no other than you. Gratitude or something deeper draws me to you and my ears are forevermore opposed to the pleadings of others. Now, stop, that will do, you are smothering me . . . take your hand away.'

'Don't run away from me, you wicked girl.'

'It is time for me to go,' I said, as I rose to join the company in the park. He assented and I amused myself, romping with the sisters. Dom Delabrise, however, followed me wherever I went, now and then sighing, which told me he rather wished that we were alone.

I was with him for a few minutes before he left and allowed him to embrace me but once. My cousin was well pleased with my conduct and she exacted another promise that I would lead him on a little longer.

I will here describe the park, as it will be the scene of a number of actions, which will be described later.

It was a spacious area, with a lot of shady trees and bushes, vines and a kitchen garden, so nicely distributed that any fancy would be suited.

Directly behind the vineyard was a pavilion. Its only apartment was one large room which derived its light from two windows. A large double door made the lattice work; for furniture it had two sofas and a few armchairs. The armchairs were so constructed that by lowering their backs they formed two beds of comfortable size; the springs were rather the worse for wear but still they were not so bad, considering the wear they were put to.

At each corner of the room was a small closet and in each closet a cot, strong and durable. The latticed door led to a terrace at each end of which was a pond with fresh, clear water. Trees surrounded this pond, giving bathers protection from the hot rays of the sun.

Behind the porch was a meadow surrounded by a thick hedge of elm trees. This was the favourite retreat of the loving couples and many were the sacrifices offered to Venus, that insatiable goddess. There was hardly a tree which could not tell of the homages paid to the frail goddess under its shade.

I for one was enchanted with this retreat and I explored it over and over. When we were about to leave it, my cousin pointed out to me the place where I was to conceal myself the day on which Suzanne was to be initiated.

Dom Bigot returned the following day and immediately sought Agatha to find out from her how she had succeeded in appeasing the wrath of his beloved.

'May I ask what success you had in conducting my case with Suzanne?'

'I succeeded far beyond my expectations.'

'What is that you say? Can it be possible that Suzanne will receive me?'

'She will receive you with pleasure, and you have everything to hope.'

'Oh, tell me all, I pray of you, do not deceive me.'

'Directly after your departure, I went to Suzanne and reasoned and pleaded with her. I made her see that her conduct towards you was harsh in the extreme and that any other in your place would have ended it right there. She received my words in a way that surprised me beyond doubt that she loves you, and if she has not yielded to you it is because she fears that you might lose control of yourself and would not be sufficiently able to protect her against conception.'

'How much I am indebted to you! How can I ever repay you for your kindness? I have a new lease on life.'

'She will probably enter a few objections, but push your cause and she will be yours.'

'Suzanne will yield! I can no longer contain myself!'

'Contain yourself nevertheless and do not make any proposals before dinner; you would not have sufficient time and you might hurt your chances. Present yourself to the Abbess and do not let anyone see by your actions that you are up to something; after dinner, I will take Suzanne to the room under some pretext and then you may come in and I will retire. It is time for us to part now, so goodbye. I am glad to have been of service to you.'

After dinner I did not fail to station myself where I could see and hear everything and, shortly after, I was delighted to see Suzanne and Agatha make their appearance.

'Why have you brought me here, Agatha?' said Suxanne. 'I did not take notice where you were taking me, I will not stay here, he can see me in the parlour or the park.'

'Under the circumstances, when you are to become reconciled, nothing should trouble you.'

'You are a wicked girl. Well, what did he say? Is his love still so warm?'

'He accosed me like a man who is torn between love and despair, but no sooner had I told him that you were willing to see him again than he became a different man; he could hardly contain himself for joy.'

'I will meet him with pleasure. He was in my thoughts all night long, and now I have nothing to fear, for here I know I cannot escape him. You make me laugh with your reasoning.

'To speak sincerely, I think I am going to yield and I fear, you know what. I dread he may be too large for me.'

'Oh, you simpleton, do you not know that in coition the woman's part usually assumes a size large enough to take in the man's without any great suffering. I was equally struck with the size of Dom de la Platierre's instrument, but I suffered ever so little when he took my maidenhead and I felt so good when he was pushing it in that I was grieved beyond measure when he took it out again. The only regret I have today is that it is not twice its size, for the tighter the fit, the greater the pleasure.'

'You will tell me all about it; I hear someone coming. Dear me, it is him . . .'

'Goodbye, I will leave you.'

Dom Bigot entered and, going up to Suzanne said: 'Ah, Suzanne, have I the happiness of meeting you again?'

'Please arise; I do not like to see you this way, kneeling before me.'

'What do I hear, my pardon is assured? I must kiss those charming lips for it.'

'I cannot breathe; my, you are terrible.'

'No, I am not, my angel, I am as gentle as a lamb.'

'That will do, you crush my skirts.'

'How white and well starched!'

'Oh, you naughty man, where are you putting your hand now; stop it, I won't have it.'

'Why not, my dear; why do you oppose our mutual enjoyment? Let go my hand.' And with this, he opened his robe and pulled out a very large staff and taking her hand, said: 'See here, touch this.'

'No. No.' But at the same time he tightly held her hand on his fine prick.

'How cruel you are, I am crazy with impatience.'

'How are you going to . . .?'

'I will take into consideration your fears, and you shall not suffer in the least, come . . . now let me . . . I cannot wait.'

'Oh, how hard you throw me on the bed; leave my skirts down, I tell you.'

'Oh, what thighs, so white and firm. Did mortal ever see such a beautiful cunt? Oh, why have you made me wait so long.'

'Oh, it is too big. You hurt me, you tear me apart, it will never go in. Oh! Oh! How you hurt . . . oh!'

'A little patience, it must go in and it . . . goes . . . in . . . at . . . last . . . at l-a-s-t!'

'Oh, Bigot, my dear friend — I am c-o-m-i-n-g . . . oh . . . how nice. Oh, Bigot, I, I . . . love you.'

'Oh, Suzanne, kiss me, hold me tight, move your arse faster . . . faster, oh, ah, ah . . .'

'Now, look what you have done, I am all wet.'

'Give me a kiss, Suzanne, dear, you see I have been careful not to deposit my semen where it might cause trouble.'

'I have been a goose to deprive myself so long of so much pleasure. I will never refuse you any more, but let us rest a while now. Let me look at that queer tool of yours. Let me examine how it is made, but do you know that at the start it hurts like fury and only my love for you made me submit to the pain your lance was putting me to?'

'And afterwards?'

'Towards the last it gave me a great deal of pleasure, well compensating me for what I had suffered at the start.'

'Come, lay down again and spread your legs apart, so, that's right. Your cunt is wide open now and from now on, only pleasure will be your share in copulating, otherwise called fucking.'

'Now, easy . . . slowly . . . it hurts a little when your prick enters, now it is all right.'

'Ah, dear little Suzanne, your tight little cunt feels heavenly around my prick.'

'Hold me a minute, Bigot, my leg is cramped . . . all right, now.'

'How do you like it, now? Do I fuck you right, love?'

'Yes, dear; but how pressed you must be, you fucked too fast. I cannot keep pace with you . . . there . . . you have done already, could you not hold out a little longer?'

'I did not hurt you very much that time?'

'No, my pleasure was greater than I ever dreamt it could be, only you left me behind this time, another time try and be slow until you see that it also overcomes me, or better still, let me tell you when to increase the tempo of your stroke. We can make it last longer then, but your prick is shrinking up, hold on; I will stiffen him again.'

'Oh, you are an adorable girl; how your cunt works that prick of mine, your muscles inside are just playing with it, it feels as if a hand was frigging it, oh, glory, hallelujah, it is stiffening up, do you feel it, dear?'

'Yes, it is living again, that big snake inside of me, but you lecherous fellow, your hands are roaming everywhere, what do you think of that backside of mine for a pair of cymbals; there is plenty to get hold of, is there not? Oh, you cochon, but it feels fine to have your finger in my arsehole.'

'I adore the beauty and size of your arse and you certainly will make a worthy priestess of Venus, an expert performer in all the different ways of making love, my pet.'

'Enough talking; now act, you are in condition again, so let us do it once more and then we will rest.'

Dom Bigot, to prolong his own as well as his partner's ecstasy, kept himself well in control, he treated her to long, strong, but slow, pushes and managed to make Suzanne spend several times without losing his own seed, working up the naturally lascivious nature of his partner to an erotic fury which found expression in the wanton movements of her arse and the obscene words she continually uttered to the intense delight of Dom Bigot.

Finally, after several spasms of delight, they glued their lips together and now Bigot let fire with all his might and after a number of very rapid strokes, they both spent and for a few minutes lay motionless and still. Then, after indulging in several glasses of wine, they fell asleep in each other's arms.

This refreshment was of great benefit to them. The attitude they assumed in going to sleep, pleased me greatly. Their legs were entwined, her hand was holding his staff of life, his hand was on her grotto of love, their partly opened mouths were near together, they seemed to breathe but one breath.

Never was a more beautiful pair than Suzanne, who was not yet twenty, and Dom Bigot, who was barely five and twenty.

Watching them, I cursed the lawmakers here below who could so cruelly make laws against a sensible and real pleasure such as this was.

I left them sweetly sleeping in each other's arms and

started to go into the park, when an unforeseen event, caused a sudden change in my plans.

Just at the entrance of the park I heard the sound of voices, I stopped to listen and, looking towards the spot whence the voices came from, I saw the Abbess' chambermaid and a strange manservant. Soon I became aware of what was going to be done. The show had just commenced when I became an interested spectator.

The aforesaid manservant had one hand under Rosalie's skirts and with the other hand he was hugging her for further orders. Rosalie was not slow in doing her best to repay the compliment. I heard him ask her to come into the park. It would be better there, he said, they would be more comfortable in one of the shady bowers. 'There is no convenience here and I do not like to fuck standing up.'

'Oh, no,' said Rosalie, 'Someone might see us; wait, I will get into a position that will enable you to get at me best.' So saying, she put her head against the wall and jutted out her rump in a most advantageous manner.

There was no delay on his part. He quickly divested himself of everything but his white vest and shirt, which he tucked up around his waist, showing the lower part of his body and his battery ready for the attack.

He got at her from behind and soon his rammer was sheathed up to the hilt. After treating her for a few minutes to slow, deliberate strokes his movement began to slacken.

'Hold back a little, Rosalie,' he whispered. 'Let us try to get through together.'

He stopped a moment or two but soon began again with redoubled vigour.

'I am coming,' cried out Rosalie. 'And here it is from me,' cried the footman, as he was getting into the short digs, then came a few spasmodic jerks, one long shove and all was over.

I could see by the twitching of their thighs and legs that they were enjoying the supreme pleasure as she felt herself backed up tight against the belly of her stallion.

They rested, letting their instruments soak in the plentiful spendings of each other. Master Jacques unsheathed his tool covered with spunk. He seemed to have lost confidence in his copulating powers, for when Rosalie showed by unmistakable signs that her appetite was not yet appeased, he cried for mercy, saying:

'Wait until evening. I am tired now; tonight in the park we will be more at our ease.' After putting themselves in order they again took a stroll in the park. I did likewise, staying there nearly an hour. Then I went back to take a look at the two lovers. They were still in nearly the same attitude that I had left them. Agatha entered a few minutes later and slapped Suzanne's arse and pulled the Reverend Father's nose.

'It is you, is it?' she said, as she awoke, and the amusing part of it was that the fair lady, feeling ashamed, hid her face in her hands and at the same time made a grand display of her arse and cunt. Bigot threw his arms around her and embraced her warmly.

'What do you say to it now?' asked Agatha.

'Look,' replied Suzanne, 'what havoc he has caused, but I don't fear him any longer. He can fuck me whenever and as often as he pleases, the more the better.'

'Ah, how you excite me!' put in the brave priest. He began to finger her but soon, thinking of something better, he pulled her to the edge of the bed and putting her legs on his shoulders, he took straight aim and drove his dagger home. She withstood the onslaught most admiringly, not in the least abashed by the presence of

Agatha, who was applauding and urging him on with
cries like:

'That is the way . . . get there! Lively . . . harder . . .
fuck that fresh cunt, let her have it strong and hard . . .
that's right . . . drive it into her up to the womb, fuck
her!'

And Suzanne, whether it was to please her companion
or her salacious self, paid him back tit for tat, move for
move. Then, taking him by the chin, she pulled his face
towards her, letting her tongue protrude far between his
lips, inviting him to suck it. Both would have liked to
prolong the struggle, but the crisis came too soon, amidst
spasmodic heaves and long-drawn sighs.

Agatha, after giving them time to regain their breaths,
announced that there was company in the abbey.

'Who is there?' asked Suzanne.

'Cimbreau, the canon, and two officers of dragoons.
Felicity has made the acquaintance of the canon and the
prioress and Rosa have taken charge of the officers. Last
year they were very intimate, so arrange your clothing
and come; you will be interested.'

As soon as I heard this, I went to see the prioress and
her friends. I was made the recipient of much attention
on the part of the three gentlemen. I was especially
admired by the canon, whose compliments were profuse.

Agatha and Suzanne, after getting Dom Bigot away,
came and joined us. My cousin drew me aside and asked
me to get Suzanne to share her bed with me, which she
agreed to without hesitation. I knew what this meant.

We all supped together and, after supper, we arranged
a party for the benefit of the good old lady.

Rosa and one of the officers left the room together;
it was then about eleven o'clock. I suspected they were
up to something, so in an offhand way I told Suzanne

that I had something to do and if she would kindly wait for me I would be back shortly.

The chamber that served for these gallant tête-à-têtes was not far off, and although it was now dark, it would serve their purpose better than the park; I was not mistaken and quietly drew near and overheard their conversation.

'Do not scold me, sweetheart,' said the officer. 'I did not think it would be so long before I could see you again. I counted the days until the order came for us to return home with our regiment.'

'You are great rovers, you soldiers. You roam about from place to place, all the time. At least you might let me hear from you, if you cannot come to see me.'

'What about you? I would also like to hear from you when I am away, but let us make better use of the time that we can be together, than to reproach each other. I want to gaze on your hidden charms and give the poor thing between my legs a chance to revel in your hermitage, so small and cute. How silky is the moss that grows along these avenues. Oh, how I love to feel the quivering flesh of a woman.'

'You ought to know my heart, Byron. Remember last year when you told me my rump was like the canon of the holy church.'

'Exactly, you have a beautiful rump and your neck has no equal in form. Yes, you were very kind and obliging to me last year, and I hoped you enjoyed yourself as well as I did.'

'I certainly showed by my behaviour that I did.'

They exchanged a few more kisses and then Rosa invited him to take coffee with her next morning in that very room.

I hastened away and rejoined the company.

I slept that night with Suzanne, who was very pleasant company till we fell asleep. The next morning I went to see how Rosa and her soldier were getting along with their coffee. I judged by the state of their clothing that one combat had already been fought. Rosa was sitting on the foot of the bed, arms and shoulders bare, while the baron drank out of her cup. I noticed that the baron's tool was standing forth in all its glory.

The coffee drunk, his ever-ready hand began to play on her instrument, then he turned the fair nun around and examined, to his own as well as her satisfaction, the abode of carnal pleasure.

Then, begging her to remain in that position, he rammed his prick into the willing cunt of the salacious nun.

It surprised me with what vigour and abandon they finished the act and I feared the consequences for Rosa, but I have found out since that when such love encounters follow themselves in succession, they are entirely harmless, for the discharge after the third assault is but thin water, incapable of producing a germ.

These two fortunate lovers did not give up the combat till both had had a surfeit of pleasure. I had seen enough. I went in search of my cousin, I found her still in bed and was questioning her how she had spent the previous night when the prioress entered.

'What, still in bed, little woman?'

'Yes, I am very tired; that horrid canon would not let me close an eye all night. Did you come for me? Wait a moment, I will be ready.'

Two Franciscans had arrived at the abbey, Dom de la Platierre and another strange monk. It was a happy event for Agatha. She found occasion to absent herself before dinner and in the afternoon had the pleasure of entertaining her lover and his friend, one after the other and then both together, one taking the legitimate road and the other occupying the neighbouring premises in her arsehole.

Dom de la Platierre, as a matter of courtesy, took the sodomitic quarters. I devoted a part of the afternoon to answering a letter which I received from Dom Delabrise; his letter follows:

Mademoiselle:

You cannot imagine my feelings since I last saw you. I do not know what to make or think of it. A thousand different thoughts are crossing my mind. What have I done to be treated thus? Everything I said was treated by you as a huge joke; I am suffering.

Now, if you really do not disdain me, why do you act so? I am not entirely ignorant of what has taken place between my confreres and the sisters and I am as interested as they are to keep the secret. I know that they are happy. Why should I be the unhappy one?

If you were not going to embrace a religious life, like myself, I would be obliged to take some kind of action. I do not know myself. But we will soon both be members of the same religious order, so why not make our hearts one?

When my studies are over I will attach myself to the same monastery where I am now and I will be able to give you frequent proofs of my love and devotion. For heavens sake, take pity on me. I am waiting impatiently for your answer and I am and always will be,

Your slave,

DOM DELABRISE

This letter really touched my heart and I answered as follows:

Monsieur:
I cannot persuade myself that you conceived the idea that I ridiculed all those gracious things that you said to me.

Why were you so greedy? If I avoided you, it was because you were arousing in me the same passions that were consuming you and I well knew that if I did not flee, I would lose all my self-control. You are welcome to come any time and be convinced.

Adieu, till we meet again,

ANGELICA

I read my letter over and saw I was giving him a pretty good hold on me, but considering everything, I decided to let it go.

All that I had seen had made such an impression on me that I could not wait. Our guests remained for three days at the abbey and nothing was spared to make their stay agreeable.

The day of their departure the younger Franciscan handed me a letter and box from Father Anselmo. Quickly withdrawing, I found the very thing he had promised me, a medium-sized dildo covered with skin and mounted with silver, and containing everything for its operation. His letter stated his regret that he was obliged to depart without seeing me once more and his hope to be more fortunate on his return.

Felicity and myself retired to our room. As soon as we were seated she asked how I was progressing with my love affair. I showed her the last letter I had received from Dom Delabrise and told her what I had answered.

'Yes, my child, it is as I expected. The scenes which you have witnessed in the last few weeks have ripened you and you are longing for the delights of copulation and your health will suffer if the sacrifice of your maidenhead is delayed much longer. And as you seem to have Dom Delabrise well in hand and he is devoted to you, it has been decided by the prioress and myself that Dom Delabrise, who will be here tomorrow, shall have the pleasure of plucking your maidenhead and introducing you to the joys of being well fucked; does that meet with your approval?'

'Yes, dear cousin, I cannot wait the time. I have been suffering from the want of consolation a strong man can give a poor woman. I thank you very much for procuring me this bliss so soon.'

'Good. Then hold yourself in readiness to receive him tomorrow afternoon, but do not think that all will be smooth sailing. You will have to undergo some pain, but of course, you know that; bear it bravely and joy will soon reward your suffering.

'Remember, too, that you must not let him spend inside of you for at least the first three times. I will caution him myself to take care of that.'

The following day my cousin pointed out to me that it would be best to rest well before the final actions were taken. I would experience more satisfaction and be in better condition to undergo the operation without the least trouble.

Finally evening came and with it Dom Delabrise. We greeted each other in a formal way, as everybody was watching us. We sat down to supper and after supper we had a stroll in the park, during which he managed to rouse my feelings to the highest pitch of erotic excitement. He led me to a seat and, kneeling down in front of me, he

put his hand under my clothes. My legs spread to give
his fingers room to explore all my hidden charms. Soon
he made me lift up my dresses. Drawers I had already
taken off on the advice of Felicity.

'Oh, dear Angelica,' he said, 'you have such a beautiful
little cunt. I must kiss it.' I felt his tongue licking and
sucking at the top of the love chink. He soon had me
afire. I pressed his head with one hand and, leaning down,
tried to find his tool.

He took notice and managed to get it out of his trousers
and put it into my eager hand. It felt as big as my arm.
I pressed and fingered it and this excited me so that I paid
my tribute in a plentiful shower.

After letting me rest for a while, my lover jumped to
his feet and said: 'Come, dear, let us go to your rooms,
I must possess you now or I shall waste what by right
belongs to you.'

I was only too eager and we hastened as fast as we
could to reach my room. My cousin greeted us there with
a smile and said: 'I will only help you undress and then
I will withdraw until tomorrow morning. I hope by that
time you will have been made a woman,' She began to
undress me and, after having stripped me to the skin, she
rendered my lover the same service. Going to the
wardrobe, she brought out a perfumed bottle of oil and,
taking his tool in her hand, applied a generous dose all
over it. Then, turning to me, she greased the holy of holies
and with the words: 'Dom Delabrise, I have done all I
could to make your path smooth and slippery, get into
her and do not spare her salacious little cunt,' she retired.

Hardly had the door closed when my lover placed me
in the position he thought best for the work in hand. He
laid me across the bed, with my arse on the edge, then
he put one pillow under me, spread my legs as far apart

169

as possible and, getting between them, he placed his prick at the entrance and tried to force his way in. He got the head in and stuck; he gently moved back and forwards, steadily pressing inwards and gaining ground slowly but surely, while I suffered immense pain under the stretching that my cunt had to undergo. But I suppressed as much as I could all signs of suffering.

Dom Delabrise said: 'Dear, have only a little patience, you will soon feel only pleasure, your pain will vanish. I will draw back a little . . . now in again. Ah, delicious! I feel your hymen; I must go through that, then you know only pleasure will be your share. I am swelling up more; the thought of taking a maidenhead is too exciting; I must go in now or I will spend before I have ravished you, you little angel.' And with this he began to push with all his might and, drawing his tool nearly entirely out of me, he returned to the attack with a mighty shove. I felt something tear within me and his big prick was in to the hilt. I fainted and when I came to again, I found Dom Delabrise busy inspecting my lacerated cunt and applying some water to it, washing off the bloody traces of my virginity.

He looked up and seeing me smile, he jumped up and kissed me rapturously. Then laying me lengthwise on the bed, he got in beside me and sucked the nipples of my bosoms and soon the amorous desires overcame all fear of pain. Getting hold of his ever-ready prick, I pulled him on top of me.

He was soon in me and treated me at first to slow, then ever-quickening movements, which soon brought on a plentiful spend of my love juice; he followed suit, but when he felt it coming he pulled out his prick and spurted it all over me from my cunt to my neck. As soon as the last drop was out, he drove the still stiff prick in again, so as to get the cunt used to its visitor, as he expressed himself. He repeated the same action twice more in succession and finally, overpowered from sheer exhaustion, we both fell asleep.

In the morning, I was all ready for poking again and my lover set to work with a vim that made me sigh with pleasure. This time we – at least I – really enjoyed to the full the delightful actions and experienced an entire feeling of satisfaction and contentment.

I was plied with all kinds of questions and everyone wanted to hear a complete account of my defloration.

Sunday evening we all repaired to the pavilion to prepare for the formal initiation of Suzanne. The actors, to the number of six, met in the parlour at seven o'clock; they were soon joined by their mistresses. The door was locked and bolted and, after embracing one another, we drank some spiced chocolate. We were ordered to disrobe and were soon in a state of complete nakedness, during which we all regarded each other.

Suzanne was led in. The two little mounds of her breasts were firm as ivory and white as alabaster, and the two crimson buttons a feast for the eyes.

We were all sworn to the rules of the order; never to divulge anything we may see, hear or do in the meetings.

A bed was then brought forth and Suzanne was placed on it. Then we were each instructed to take a partner and arrange ourselves on cots close by and await the word of the prioress.

This soon come. 'Get ready, Dom Bigot, and do your duty by Suzanne and we will follow suit.' No sooner said than done. Suzanne suffered the introduction of the big prick of her lover without a murmur and soon the rocking and poking became general.

Suzanne and Dom Bigot got out of their bed and

received the congratulations of their confreres.

After a little rest, each chose a partner for the second act of this lustful drama. They wished to offer, all at the same time, their noble sacrifice, to the goddess who presided over all their pleasures and they finally drowned their instruments in streams of spunk.

The prioress, while being fucked, amused herself by handling the pricks of two fathers standing on each side of her, to give more ardour to the champion screwers. Each held across his lap one of the nuns, as one would hold a child about to be chastised.

Suzanne was stationed between these two batteries, belly to the front, thighs apart, two fingers holding open her pretty little snatch. Agnes and the parish priest were doing it dog fashion.

The prioress was far from satiated, for she called de la Platierre to lie on his back. She mounted him and then called to de la Motte, offering him her arsehole to bugger, and, calling the Franciscan, she made him stand in front of her while she licked and sucked his prick.

After this sweet enjoyment, at which I had shed my love juice times without number, we all returned to our rooms for much-needed rest.

I leave you to imagine what must have been my feelings after witnessing the scenes before described, being very young and possessing strong sexual passions.

Reaching my room, I threw myself on the bed and fell asleep. I cannot say how many stiff pricks I saw in my dreams. They were of all sizes and shapes and they made such an impression upon me that I awoke with a start, burning with sexual desire. Involuntarily I began to rub and press and finger my itching cunt, until a discharge brought relief.

Then, getting up, I partook of some light refreshments and went to the park again. It was about six o'clock. I saw the Society approaching and went to meet them; the ladies smiled pleasantly and the gentlemen passed some complimentary remarks.

I asked my cousin to tell the professor that I wished to speak to him and he hastened to my side. We entered one of the stalls and he asked me kindly what he could do for me. I asked him as a favour to let Dom Delabrise visit on the following Wednesday.

'With all my heart, my dear girl,' he replied, 'your wish will be granted. Who on earth could refuse anything to such a charming girl? You have the privilege of seeing him as often as you wish, but for the sake of appearance you must be cautious. However, you won't have to reproach me on that score.

'And will you promise me something in return? That you will meet me in some quiet corner and I will come expressly to see you. Try and have the key to the pavilion and I will write and let you know on what day I can be at your service. Now be sure and don't disappoint me.'

He embraced me again and then, hearing the bell calling us to supper, we went in. All our guests had departed save Dom de la Platierre.

We remained at table much longer than usual in order to amuse the Abbess but as the conversation ran along very dull subjects, everybody was glad to retire when the sign was given.

On finding ourselves alone in our room, my cousin asked me if I had seen everything that had taken place.

I told her that I had not, for I had left about the time that Dom Bigot had finished. 'Then you missed the best part of it,' she said.

'What in the name of God could you have done more?' I asked.

She described other parts of the ceremony of taking the vows of chastity with which I was about to become acquainted at my own initiation and which I will describe then.

Until the arrival of my lover, I passed most of the time in the company of the ladies, who now gave me their full confidence. At last the long looked-for day arrived.

Dom Delabrise came straight to my room. Very little time was lost in cooing and loving; he had my skirts up in less time than it takes to describe it. He pushed his noble prick with one shove up to the hilt and fucked me beautifully twice in succession.

The night passed in a way you may imagine and we did not leave the bed until late the next day.

At about three o'clock in the afternoon we repaired to the garden, I having possessed myself of a key.

The day being very warm, we made our way to the fountain, which seemed so cool and nice that we soon divested ourselves of our clothing and proceeded to take a bath. After the bath we concluded that an offering to the god of love would be just the thing.

I had told him of the various postures that the ladies had assumed at the reception given to Suzanne and we tried a few. For instance, I made him fuck me dog fashion, which I enjoyed very much, as it seemed to me that his prick was penetrating me further than ever before; then we tried a St George and finally the wheelbarrow act was given a trial.

However, as pain follows pleasure, we finally were forced to part. A messenger came to inform me that I was wanted in the parlour, so, kissing my lover, I hurried off to see what was wanted of me. On reaching the parlour, a woman handed me a letter. I broke the seal and read as follows:

Sweetheart:

I will meet you in the pavilion this evening at nine o'clock. Try to bring Suzanne with you. The strange Bernardino is very much in love with her and cannot make up his mind to leave without seeing her once more. I know she will come when she knows who is there. Take care to conceal this from everybody else. In pleasant anticipation, I am,

Your humble servant,

P—

I showed the letter to Suzanne and she seemed quite surprised. Then, recovering herself, she whispered:

'Ah, Father Grignolet, just what I want. You shall fuck me to your heart's content. He has such a fearful big tool; I was already longing to have it shoved into me at the reception.'

We agreed to meet then at the appointed place. I then took my cousin into the secret, as I kept nothing from her.

After throwing on a few light wraps we went to the place. Hearing a knock, I motioned to Suzanne to conceal herself, just to make the other gentleman a little anxious, then I went and opened the door. They entered eagerly and Dom Grignolet, casting an eager glance around the room and not seeing Suzanne, asked with every sign of disappointment:

'Where is she?'

'She could not come,' I answered, but Suzanne burst out laughing and was soon discovered.

'So this is the way you two tease people!' he cried, as he gave her a warm hug.

It was a lovely night, so we went and sat down on the edge of the meadow. I soon held the royal baton in my hand but I raised some objection to submitting to the principal object of our meeting, so he proceeded to calm my fears by kissing me and assuring me that it was not so monstrous after all.

'See,' said he, 'I will go nice and easy, and it will not hurt you a bit.'

With a few words of encouragement from Suzanne, I let him have his way. He began by pushing lightly at the entrance, which invisibly opened, letting it slip in clear to the hilt then, making no further effort to control himself, he gave himself up to the fullest enjoyment of a passionate fucking. His movements, becoming faster and faster, were nearly equalled by my own and the supreme crisis came to us at nearly the same moment.

'See,' he said as he treated my cunt to another vigorous lunge, 'I got through in great shape and you also, little one. You know how to wriggle your arse to get there. Ah, that's the way. Squeeze tight. Oh, that's nice. I'm stuck on that juicy cunt of yours.'

Grignolet and his companion were not so quick as we were, and they were making desperate efforts to catch up.

'Look,' I said to the professor, 'See the full moon bobbing up and down,' referring of course to the big white arse of Grignolet, which trembled with suppressed emotion, so to speak.

Catching sight of an apple lying in the grass I made a dive for it, and, taking straight aim, I hit the bull's eye between the two fat cheeks of Grignolet's arse. This made us laugh but he, without stopping or losing a stroke, cried: 'Stop your nonsense!'

After a few more strokes they came to a finish. Hours are but minutes when one is making love of this sort, and midnight was upon us before we knew it. So we proposed to the two gentlemen to make use of the two beds that were in the pavilion and that we would keep them company until morning.

They readily agreed to this and, the night being warm, we stripped. As the professor showed inclinations to take another turn, I took a kneeling position on the bed and he, understanding what was wanted, mounted me and drove his long prick into my hungry cunt from behind. I felt it pushing against my womb and this was decidedly the best fuck yet, though it tired me, and as soon as we both had spent, we fell asleep with the agreement of repeating the same performance in the morning.

The sun was already high when we awoke and the first thing that we did was to make an all around examination of our genitals, which naturally fired us to a repetition of the previous night's deeds. While the professor was engaged in doing it to me in the same fashion as the night before, Grignolet entered the room and said:

'Ah, my brother, you seem to be very well served by this young girl.'

'Yes indeed, and how is it with your partner?'

'Fine, very fine; it could not be better. They say that enjoyment kills desire, but with me it seems to be born over again right away. I have no doubt that you are in accord with me, for your sweetheart is also most charming. Now that I think of it, I must make her pay for that prank of throwing the apple at my arsehole. I am sure I have another charge left.' As the professor just then ejected his seed all over my buttocks and withdrew, he quickly took his place and treated me to a vigorous fucking, which I enjoyed to the utmost.

But I called to the professor and Suzanne to come to my assistance and slap this impudent arse while he was fucking me, which they did, thereby increasing the force of his strokes which formed a delightful diversion for the onlookers. This ended, we sent our friends away well satisfied.

The following Monday the Society gave another reception. I remained in my room and put Dom Delabrise through his paces.

A few days later the young Franciscan kept his word with Agatha. His return was the signal for launching into some new and varied amusements. She kept him in her own room during the first day of his arrival, in order that her companions might not see him and also that she might carry out the scheme that she had planned for just such an occasion.

The next day she sought me and said:

'Listen, Angelica, you must help me to disguise my young Franciscan, the one who gave you a letter for me about a month ago. You remember? He is in my room now and I want to pass him off for my niece. I will bet anything the ladies will not know the difference. Oh, what a lot of fun we will have.

'He is just small enough to pass for a pretty young miss of eighteen or twenty. Your clothes will just about fit him and everything will pass off all right, if you will only promise to hold your tongue.'

'Don't worry about me, I will play my part all right. I think my cousin is not there now so I will run down to my room and bring up the dresses. Just wait for me a moment.'

I soon returned, loaded down with petticoats, waists, skirts and chemises, drawers; everything, even shoes and stockings. The young Franciscan was there and hurried to relieve me of my burden, thanking me at the same time most graciously.

'I know I shall do something that will betray me,' he said.

'Do exactly as we tell you,' said Agatha, 'and there will be no chance of it; your voice is soft and sweet and there is not a sign of hair on your face, so I do not see why . . .'

'I won't be able to keep from laughing all the same.'

I pretended to leave, but Agatha told me to come back as she would soon have need of my assistance, so I left the room noiselessly, retraced my steps, and knelt down in front of the door, to listen to what was going on between the two.

First I heard the voice of Agatha saying: 'Take off everything, why don't you?'

'What! My shirt too?'

'Why certainly; here is one for you to put on. Oh, the poor dear, how odd he looks, it is just too comical, oh, my . . . oh, my . . .'

'What do you mean, me or John Thomas? If you mean the latter all I have to say is, he is quiet now but it will not do to arouse him. I will not answer for anything he does then, for he has a head of his own.'

'Never mind that, I have had my fill. Well, how awkward you are, here, not that way . . . there, that is better . . . hold on . . . straighten the skirt a little, now the sleeve, so. Your breast is too flat, we have to puff it out that way. Now for the hair, I wish Angelica were here to help me.'

'So her name is Angelica. She seemed to be a very nice, sociable young lady.'

'You seem to take to her.'

'Your kind favours are quite enough for me as long as you condescend to bestow them upon me. There is small chance of my looking elsewhere for them. Does she intend to become a nun?'

'Yes, and that before very long, too. Well, the devil take the bonnet, I cannot manage it. Ah, there you are, Angelica, just in time, I cannot manage this young lady's hair; a little more and I would be tempted to swear.'

'My clothes fit him to perfection; give me that switch. Ah there, that is it. Just too sweet for anything. How pretty you look, to be sure!'

'Hold on a minute.'

'What is the matter? Have you the colic?'

'No, but I have the cramps.'

'Oh, I see, you are not used to having such a pretty maid to dress you; it seems to upset you somewhat.

'Well, Agatha, you had better treat him for the cramps. I will be back presently.' And with that I went out, running in again in about half an hour.

'Well, how is our young miss feel now? From the condition of your clothing you two must have been working with might and main to effect a cure for the cramps.' I again helped them to put themselves into a presentable shape.

A quarter of an hour afterwards the prioress entered with my cousin. Our strange young lady returned their salutations with the best of grace.

'Tell her to be seated,' said the prioress, addressing Agatha. 'Your niece seems to have caught a cold; how or when did she come? You have not told me that you expected her.' A question like this would have embarrassed an ordinary person, but not one with such a ready wit as Agatha, and the Franciscan supported her nicely in everything she said.

'I did not expect the dear girl,' said Agatha. 'She was in deep trouble, and I being her nearest relative she came here for consolation and I am delighted that she did, even if she dropped in on me so suddenly and unannounced; she got here this morning.'

While Agatha was thus pulling the wool over the eyes of her companions, the Franciscan cast down his eyes and assumed an air of deep distress and even went so far as to shed a few crocodile tears.

I had to turn my head to keep from laughing outright while the prioress consoled to the best of her ability, putting a multitude of questions to him all of which he answered in a way that would be creditable to the most accomplished liar.

'Do not grieve so, sweetheart. I know your mother will be very anxious about your sudden departure but she will feel better when she hears that you have come to this place. Tell me without concealing anything; what caused your sudden flight? I am a friend and adviser of your aunt and will be the same to you if you will let me. All I can do shall be done to make life pleasant for you while you remain here, so unburden yourself with the fullest confidence.'

'Just because a young officer called on me several times, my mother imagined . . .'

'Ah, your mother imagined that all was not right between you two?'

'Yes, and she forbade him to enter the house.'

'And that grieved you sorely?'

'Words cannot express my emotion, I cannot give you any idea of the extent of my suffering.'

'But your mother did not raise any objection until you had done something to rouse her suspicion; perhaps he acted somewhat familiarly without meaning any harm. You know, mothers are very jealous of the virtue of their daughters, so perhaps she was justified in acting as she did.'

'Yes, it is true, she caught him as he was about to kiss my hand after he had whispered a lot of sweet words in my ears.'

'Yes, yes, my suspicions were true, and when he had gone, she scolded you, I suppose.'

'Yes, a great deal; from that time on my life was made a burden to me. It nearly drove me insane when I could no longer see him; his absence was insupportable. He was ever uppermost in my mind, his many acts of kindness, his pleasant and entertaining little stories . . .'

'And I suppose you devised a way of seeing him secretly?'

'Yes, that is true. Although my mother was very strict, she was not however so blind to her own pleasures that she did not leave me alone occasionally; times which I took occasion of to smuggle him into the house. I took one of the maids into the secret and was thus able to carry on our meetings for quite a while without being discovered.

'One day we thought she was at devotions when she came upon us; I concealed him as best I could but there were always gossips about and the report soon spread that he was seen to issue from our garden at eight o'clock in the morning.'

'I suppose that it was in your bedroom that you used to hide him from prying eyes?'

'How queer you are!' interposed my cousin, 'asking such strange questions. It does not concern us where she hid him, just let her tell us what her mother said.'

'She paid me a visit while I was still in bed and pounced upon me like a tigress. I thought she was going to tear my limbs from my body. She threatened to place me in a neighbouring convent of which it was known that the inmates were treated in a very severe manner.

'I got up and dressed myself; I took only the clothes that I have on my back; I made my way to the hut of one of our tenants, which was not very distant. I remained there for the rest of the day and then made my way here to my aunt. So that is why I am here, enjoying the good fortune of your acquaintance and hospitality.'

I now had to leave the room in order to relieve my pent-up mirth, which done, I returned to help along the comedy.

'You must take your niece to pay her respects to the Abbess,' the prioress advised Agatha.

'Not yet, I want first to write to my sister and I think it best to wait till I receive her answer.'

'Well, as you think best; we must take her however, to see the house and the garden after dinner, and make the acquaintance of our friends. And you, my dear child,' she added, turning to the Franciscan, 'be at your ease and everything will come out all right.'

My cousin heartily approved, only adding that she would be pleased to have me act as companion to the newcomer. Then, bidding us adieu, they retired.

No sooner were their backs turned than we had to burst into a violent fit of laughter. Agatha congratulated the Franciscan on the excellence of his acting and the better to show her appreciation, she gave him several impulsive hugs. I felt like doing likewise but he saved me the trouble and gave me a few hearty kisses, which I most graciously accepted. Then we went to dinner, bidding him come along and make himself at home.

As there were no other visitors at the abbey that afternoon, all the ladies came to visit us, as much out of curiosity to see the niece, so-called, as to pass the time away.

The Franciscan had to answer a thousand questions, which he did in such a clever manner that none suspected his sex. The reader will wonder at this and so would I, had I not been present to see it.

After vespers we went for a stroll in the park and by and by we found ourselves in the pavilion. The Franciscan was greatly pleased with it. Then all proceeded to go in bathing, a proposition which greatly embarrassed the Franciscan, but he got out of it by pleading sickness, saying he feared taking more cold.

'Let them bathe without you,' said the prioress. 'Come over here and sit by my side to keep me company.'

We retained our chemises in order to not scandalize the pretended young miss and I noticed that his gaze was principally fixed on Suzanne and myself. I was giving full play to the round globes of my posterior so that he could observe them at his ease and out of pure vanity, on entering the water, I raised my linen so that he could see that what I had concealed there was not to be sneezed at either.

The others who entered the water showed nearly as much as I did. He was evidently not used to such sights for they soon had their effect on his masculine nature.

Agatha perceived this and whispered in my ear: 'We should at least have put drawers on him. I am sure he cannot help betraying himself.' Sure enough, the prioress, seeing how uneasily he acted, asking him if he still felt indisposed and turning, he answered: 'No.' But the one thin skirt was ill-suited to hide the cause of his uneasiness and the prioress, accidently putting her hand down, felt something thick and rigid.

'Ah, what is this!' she exclaimed. 'I believe if I am not mistaken, that . . .'

He made an effort to rise but she held him fast. 'Oh, oh, girls, come here and see what a comical young lady we have here.'

Three of them ran to see, their wet chemises drawn tight about their rumps. Agatha and I remained where we were, writhing in veritable spasms of mirth.

'Well, if this is not a nice how-do-you-do; no wonder they were so careful of him.'

My cousin came and asked me who he was and went back to tell the others.

'Ah, ah, my gay rooster! That is how you disguise yourself, so to pursue our young pullets; we will have to cut your *Corpus Delicti*.'

'Pardon him,' said Rosa. 'I pray thee, it would be too bad to deprive him of his cordon.'

'Let me catch my breath, ladies, and I will perform any penance you may impose on me.'

'Well, really,' said Suzanne, 'did you have to perform such very disagreeable ones during your apprenticeship, whenever you made some slight infractions on your saintly obligations?'

'I object to further questioning; I saw him first, so he belongs to me,' said Agatha.

'You have no longer any claim on him,' cried my cousin. 'You ought to be satisfied with the slick game you put up on us, and take it in your turn, the same as the rest of us.'

'For your sake, ladies, I wish that he was supplied with half a dozen good stiff ones,' was the comment I had to make.

'See, you were in the plot, too, my pretty miss, and I have a mind to make you pay for it all. The more I think of it, the more it surprises me, and still, who wouldn't be deceived by that sweet countenance, those childish airs and those large, innocent blue eyes? And to better deceive us he made up a well-constructed story of a supposed love affair, told with such an air of remorse and shame, I will never wonder at anything again.'

'My friends, what a white skin he has and this that I hold in my hand is no trifle, either. Believe me, Agatha, I see here a choice morsel for you which I know you will certainly appreciate.'

'Take some of it yourself while you are dressing, just to satisfy yourself of what he can do in that line.'

'That is very well,' said Suzanne, 'but are you not afraid that it will tax his strength too much? He does not look rugged, so you ought to be as sparing with him as possible.'

'True, but the young should work; it does them good. See the motion of his hind quarters, isn't it just splendid? Why, both of them are dying with rapture.'

'Yes, but not in the same condition in which you took him. It will be some time before I furnish another bird for that bush of yours, seeing how you have treated this one.'

Just then Rosa called: 'I hear some noise in the pavilion. See, there is Dom Bigot, the Vicar, and Dom de Platierre.'

'Angelica, hurry quick into the shade of the elms with our young friend here and when you have rearranged his clothes, come back here again, both of you . . . good evening, gentlemen, you are welcome, have you just arrived?'

'I should say not, we have been rapping on all the doors for the past hour without a response. We began to believe you were not here. And how are you Suzanne, you have just bathed, I presume?'

'Yes, their skins look fresh and rosy.'

'Pray be on your good behaviour, for we have with us a young lady who would be greatly shocked at the least show of impropriety.'

'She is Agatha's niece; see, here she comes with Angelica.'

'She is a beauty, no doubt about it. I would rather have her tumble into my bed than many other things that I can mention.'

'You talk as if everything was made for your especial benefit. You rascal, you cannot see a girl but you want to get between her legs then and there.'

The two monks greeted the Franciscan most cordially and made desperate attempts at gallantry, mistaking him all the while for a pretty young maid yet in her teens, and he acted the part to perfection.

The monks and most of the ladies finally departed, the prioress and Agatha remaining behind for a moment to bid me take good care of him, and to have him sleep in my cousin's room. My cousin being aware of this arrangement, slept elsewhere in order, as she said, not to discommode me and spoil our fun.

She also thoughtfully asked Agnes to bring our supper. I then returned to my young man, who said, as he greeted me with a kiss:

'I am to sleep with you?'

'Oh, no,' I said, 'you are to sleep in my cousin's room. I will have some clean linen put on her bed so that you may sleep comfortably.'

'Oh, then I am to sleep without you?'

'After all that you have been through today, and what the other ladies have accorded you, I do not wish to be too exacting. I can wait for some other time, you must be in need of a good rest.'

'I am not so tired but that I can fire a few more shots; you do not know the prowess of a votary of St. Francis.'

'Well, I do not think you have any strength left, for you had to meet a woman today who well knows how to take the starch out of a thing like that, but if you insist, you rogue, let me see if there is any life in it.'

'Yes, if you let me see that little cunt of yours. I had only a glimpse of it today as you were entering the water. My, but this is a dandy one.'

'That will do; someone is coming. Oh, it is Sister Agnes.'

'Here, I have brought you some supper. Ah, what a pretty companion you have, Angelica, and if I am not mistaken she is concealing something about her person that is against the rules.'

'Ah, I see my cousin has let you into the secret, now tell me, wouldn't you wish to have a niece like that?'

'You certainly have made a nice catch, but I do not envy you your good fortune. I wish you every enjoyment. Here, this is to restore your failing energies, so excuse me: I must be off. Goodbye.'

'That sister is a nice girl, to be sure.'

'Sit over there and let us begin our supper.'

'No, let us sit close together, but first let me take off this kerchief. You will be more comfortable. Let me uncover those beautiful titties; tell me all about them. Oh, how I long to kiss the dear little treasures.'

I made him eat a great deal of celery roots, cooked in the broth of tender spring chickens and many other delicacies.

After supper we took a stroll in the park to aid digestion. During our walk he kept up his foolishness and I did not have the heart to enter any objection. We saw the two monks and some of the sisters approaching, so we turned and went inside. We sat up a little while and then went to bed. I pretended that I did not want to sleep with him and said:

'Listen, I am as fond of this pleasure as you are, but

I know that men tire themselves sooner than we do, so do not tease me. I will give you all you want in the morning.'

'Well, I am here now, so let us talk, laugh and enjoy ourselves. Since I came stark-naked into this world, I have been blessed with a goodly share of personal charms.'

'Yes, your skin is white and very soft for a boy.'

'Perhaps it is because I am still so young and, like yourself, the only hair I have is on the top of my head or below on my belly, or maybe like a cat's a little round the tail, but as to tails, I have one of the nicest that I have ever laid eyes on.'

'Hug me again and you can feel and play with what you think will amuse you the most. I won't object, but let me sleep now and I will promise you all you want tomorrow morning.'

So we fell asleep and did not awake until ten o'clock the next morning. He was refreshed and was giving me a proof of it, when my cousin, the prioress and Agatha came in.

'Good morning, children. Just look at that young rogue, say, doesn't he seem to enjoy himself!'

'You ought to be grateful to us for getting you this lovely maid.'

'I appreciate my happiness and your kindness as also that of the other ladies here, which calls for the most sincere gratitude. My satisfaction can but change to deep sorrow when a cruel fate compels me to part from so charming a place and from such friends.'

'You are a good young man and we thank you, but listen, remember it is because you are in holy orders and your companionship is agreeable, that we have accorded you this little diversion, but no indiscretions, you understand?'

'Your words do not please me. I am young, that is true, but I know when to hold my tongue. And besides, I am an interested party and I think you are right in not denying yourself the pleasures so dear to all the world, so have no fear of what I may say or do.

'We can well say that such and such has smothered all those desires that nature has given him, I have my own opinions about the matter and I am not simple enough to follow their lead. If I had embraced this calling, I have done what many others have done before me. One must hitch onto something or other, if he doesn't know how to make the most of it, that is his fault. Therefore, ladies, I hope to be able to give you now and then a proof of my gratitude.'

'You have spoken so nicely that I am tempted to embrace you myself. You must come and see us often; you will always be welcome. Now, don't you think it is time to get up?'

I expect the reader to form anything but a good opinion of me for being unfaithful to Dom Delabrise so soon. And scanning over my conduct I must admit there are sufficient grounds for it. But I plead my youth for an excuse; I saw Dom Delabrise but once a week, so my passions, fanned by example, got the best of me.

That did not mean that the sentiments he had inspired in me had grown cold. If chance had thrown other lovers in my way, he remained always the most dearly beloved as the continuation of this story will prove.

The young Franciscan stayed four days longer and performed his penance to our entire satisfaction, promising before he left to return as soon as possible to what he termed an enchanting island. The ladies spoke frequently of him but other objects came to claim their attention, so they gradually began to forget him.

The following day I received a letter from my true love, which ran as follows:

Dearest Angelica:

We must depart tomorrow to our orders, and I cannot have the supreme pleasure of seing you this week. It is useless to describe the pain it gives me to leave thus without seeing you, for you well know what the state of my feelings must be.

One thing consoles me, however. I will only be absent for seven or eight days at the most and then I will repay myself for what I have missed this while.

The prior promised us a vacation of three days and you can imagine with whom I will spend them, but there are strings attached. Although everyone is to have a vacation, we will not all have it at the same time. We are to take it by twos and one of my friends named Vernier has asked leave to accompany me and I didn't have the heart to refuse him.

It is the same Vernier that you met last year; Rosa knows him well. He, and he only, knows what has been going on at the convent; the rest know absolutely nothing about it and the prior did not grant them permission to visit it. His coming need not worry us in the least; he can amuse himself to his heart's content. As for us, we can take care of that little matter to the king's taste.

So until we meet again, take good care of your health and I will husband my forces so that when we meet, our mutual pleasure shall be greater than ever.

Goodbye, my queen, a thousand kisses for you.
Your ever faithful and sincere friend,

DOM DELABRISE

I was glad to hear from him but I thought it most untimely and was therefore somewhat vexed. Somehow I felt that he could never be the same to me. To draw my mind from these thoughts, I went in search of Suzanne, whom I found alone.

This was a surprise to her, as she believed I was yet with my new lover; I stated the object of my visit and she asked me to take a seat and help her with some embroidery she was engaged upon, so we could talk at our leisure.

'Well, Suzanne, what is your opinion of the young Franciscan?'

'He is perfectly charming; we passed two hours together and I was delighted.'

'He is the innocent cause of much sorrow for me tonight.'

'And how so?'

'I dreamt of Dom Delabrise the other night and he reproached me most bitterly for bestowing my affections upon another, and the truth is, I have come to blame myself for my conduct.'

'Never mind what I tell you, you ought to hold Dom Delabrise dearer than any other man in the whole world, but that does not mean that he must have a monopoly.

'Take me and Dom Bigot, for instance. I love him dearly but I do not forego my pleasure on account of him. No, whenever the opportunity presents itself of getting some extra fucks, I take it, as I am sure he does too, with other women. Liberty is a beautiful thing in itself. Besides, variety is the spice of life. There are pleasures that I derive from Dom Bigot that I never would from another, because I really love him.

'By and by you will experience the same feeling with Dom Delabrise, but that should not prevent us from

taking another prick into our cunts once in a while. If
it does not give entire satisfaction, it always cools, at least
for a time, the heat of our burning slits. Besides, situated
as we are, we could hardly do otherwise. It would not
be good policy for us to give ourselves up entirely to one
man and run the risk of jealousy. When you swear
fidelity, you put shackles on your conduct.'

'Your advice is most sensible and has quieted my
scruples with regard to Dom Delabrise, but he shall
always have the warmest place in my heart, just the
same.'

'And I suppose you are not so awfully sorry that he
has not come today after all.'

'Don't let us speak about it any longer; I feel as if I
were going to . . .'

'Tut-tut, it is always best to talk about what we love
most, but when we have finished this strand, we will quit,
and do what we can to console each other.'

She then came over and sat near me, and throwing her
arms around me, she gave me an impetuous hug, then,
taking my face between her hands, she kissed me several
times; then, drawing my hand over her shoulders, she
began to work her nimble fingers through my waist until
they reached my titties, an operation that sent a thrill of
pleasure through my whole body.

She lingered, fondling first one nipple and then the
other. I could feel her knees shaking from excitement as
she tried to force her hand down on my belly, but a tight
waistband prevented her from going that far. Suddenly,
as if beside herself with desire, she pulled me down till
I lay almost across her lap and before I knew what she
wanted, I felt her hand beneath my skirts and another
spasm of delight overcame me.

Her magnetic fingers were soon playing up and down,

to and fro around my secret parts, now and then finding their way along the crack that divided my arse. ·

I became weak from sheer pleasure and rolled off her lap onto the floor, she falling on top of me; my skirts were clear up to my waist and the sight of my limbs seemed to excite her still more, if such a thing was possible.

She almost sank her teeth into the flesh of my legs and body. I rolled over on my stomach to avoid her bites, and she drove her face between the cheeks of my arse and I could feel her tongue forcing its way into my enchanted little arsehole.

I had caught the fever from her and was now subjecting her person to the same treatment.

We had wriggled into the position that knowing ones refer to as '69' – that is, our heads were buried between each other's thighs and we were licking and sucking each other's cunts so that soon the supreme spasm of spending overcame us.

I felt it flowing from me at the moment when Suzanne's slit squirted a shower of whitish liquid all over my face. The reaction now came, our muscles relaxed, our heads dropped and we held each other for a while in a limp embrace.

Then I made my cousin acquainted with the contents of the letter from Dom Delabrise. She did not seem to be much put out about the arrival of Vernier. She, on the contrary, seemed highly pleased.

One day while rummaging in her bureau, I came across a small article of a peculiar shape, covered with the hair, the same as that which ornamented my dildo.

'Say, cousin, what is this?'

'What is what, my dear?'

'This, what is it used for?'

'Oh, that is what men use when they have connection with women, to guard against children.'

'How is it that our friends never made use of them?'

'I'll tell you why. They do not use them except when they have had no fucking for some time and they fear that they cannot control themselves. At the moment of spending and to prevent any serious consequences, they put on these preventatives.'

'Has it ever been used in you?'

'Yes, but I don't mind.'

'I will put it into my pocket, to satisfy my curiosity.'

'It also serves another purpose, you know. There are women called whores, who sell their charms to the first comer. Well, the most prudent of these make use of it to guard against contagion of some sexual disease which men are sometimes afflicted with.'

'As I see, the one wears it to prevent getting knocked up and the other to ward off disease.'

'Precisely!!'

Until the arrival of Dom Delabrise, I did the best I knew how under the circumstances. Rosa, Suzanne and myself were strolling in the park when he and his friend arrived at the convent. They immediately came out in search of us, not even taking off their travelling boots.

The preliminary civilities were hardly over when Suzanne, under some pretext, hurried off in spite of our entreaties to make her stay. Rosa took charge of Vernier.

'Well, Blondy, it is a rare treat to see you!' she said, addressing him in the most familiar way. 'Don't be such a stranger after this; you must accompany your friend every time he comes.'

We paid very little attention to their lovemaking and cooing – we were too busy with our own – but when they entered one of the rooms in the pavilion, I called my lover's attention to it.

He immediately expressed a desire to do likewise, so we lost no time in getting inside. As we entered we heard the other two talking and, according to what we heard, they were just then busily engaged in inspecting each other's secret charms. Rosa was saying:

'I like your prick, because your hair and mine are of the same colour; see, there is no difference between them.'

We did not take time to amuse ourselves in the same manner. Dom Delabrise was in too much of a hurry. I had his long, stiff dart in my hands and my burning cunt was consumed with a desire to sheath it.

He made me kneel down on the bed and at once shoved his prick from behind into my hot cunt. He worked slowly and succeeded in making me come three times before he pulled out to squirt his spunk all over my arse.

I was delighted with this new way of fucking, for I felt his dear prick go in much further than before and I made up my mind that in the future I would practice this mode oftener. I told my lover so, who informed me that there were many more ways of making love, which in time he would teach me.

It being near supper time, there was just time enough for the two monks to put themselves into a respectable state to go and make their bow to the Lady Superior.

After supper I brought forth the little object of which I have spoken, wishing to try it and satisfy my curiosity. It did not take me long to make up my mind that it was of little value. I felt no agreeable sensations of it working in and out.

I managed to have Dom Delabrise with me that night and made him fuck me six times before he went to sleep. I awoke first in the morning, ready for more deeds of love, and I therefore lost no time in uncovering my lover and inspecting his sweet prick. I began to finger it and had the satisfaction of getting it into working condition, when my lover awoke. I turned and offered him my altar from behind. He understood and gave me another dose dog-fashion, as he called it.

Just then my lover's chum entered and, seeing how we were employed, wanted to retire, but my lover as well as myself, as if calling from one mouth, called to him to stay.

'Don't be bashful,' said Dom Delabrise. 'You will enjoy this picture. Angelica dear, frig his prick while I keep on fucking you and then you may have him in your cunt after I am done.'

I pulled the prick of Vernier out of his trousers. I found it already stiff and the sight excited me to the highest pitch of lasciviousness. I felt myself coming but instead of causing my excitement to abate, the lewd proceedings kept me in fighting trim. Delabrise shot his spunk all over my arms and made room for his friend, who entered me in the same position. He managed to make me come twice before he let his load fly. I, in the meantime, fingered my lover's prick and stiffened it up again.

I treated him to a furious frigging, which caused him to spend all over my hand and face. Then we got up, satisfied for the time, and went to recover ourselves with a rich breakfast.

My cousin received company in the parlour that day and I had the room all to myself and was able to make my lover's stay a continued round of pleasure.

I had Suzanne in with me and Vernier was also of the party, and between myself and Suzanne, we succeeded in keeping the two monks in continuous excitement. We made them perform wonders of fucking and when they finally had to leave us, they did so with the knowledge that they had spent a delightful vacation, even though we had completely drained them.

The following Thursday, Dom Delabrise returned and it was, as far as I was concerned, the worst possible time he could have chosen, for I was very much indisposed, as my monthly period had just come around.

I informed him of the matter, which ill-fitted the special purpose he had come for. He was very much put out by this mischance. No sooner were we in our bedroom than he renewed his lamentations. I tried to reason with him but it was of no avail. He even went so far as to try to take the fortress by storm and did not desist until I had promised to do my best to quench his passions in some other way.

'Ah, my poor man, how you must suffer, let me put my hand into your trousers and see what is the matter – hm – but it is hard. I think I know a cure for it, though. Lie on the bed . . . that's it . . . you know that I do not mean to be unkind. There, how do you like this? Does my tongue tickle it nicely? Now I will take it into my mouth and suck it like a baby sucks the mother's breast. Tell me, pet, does it make you feel good?'

'Yes, yes, darling, keep on, don't stop, dear. You were always kind to me, I love you more than ever, you sweet little sucker . . . keep . . . keep on . . . let me move it in your sweet mouth . . . ah! that is nice . . . a little more . . . Oh! Oh! I am c-o-m-i-n-g.'

I swallowed the cream and found it delicious. Then I made him button up, as I expected my cousin to enter any moment.

We had supper and then I proposed to share my bed with him. He was still thanking me for the pleasure I had given him when my cousin entered and I told her in whispers about my indisposition and that he would like to have her in my stead, but didn't dare to ask her.

'Willingly. Did he think I would refuse? I would indeed be hard to please if I did not accept an offer like this.'

She ate supper with a particular relish that evening. I left them to themselves. Finally they stripped and went to bed. I bid them good night and wished them all kinds of pleasure, then I went to bed.

I prepared breakfast and served it to them while yet in bed. During the afternoon we found ourselves entirely alone. I suggested that Dom Delabrise should tell us how old he was and under what circumstances he had had his first connection with a woman.

'I was seventeen and had already entered our order when I gave up my maidenhead to a girl of sixteen and she made me a present of hers, and it happened in this way:

'The young girl was my cousin. She was left an orphan while still very young. My mother took and raised her with us. I left home to enter the order of White Monks. While there, I learned many things from my young companions and among other things was a knowledge of the relation of the sexes, so that in case a girl fell into my power, I could fuck her without further instructions, even with as much skill as Brother Luce performed on Sister Agnes.

'After being formally enrolled, I was permitted to pay a visit to my home. My brother was away studying and my sister was married, so I found nobody at home but my parents and my cousin.

'I hardly knew her, so much had she changed, but it was a change decidedly to her advantage. I noticed from the fullness of her bosom that she was no longer a child and I resolved then and there that I would deflower her.

199

'My mother furnished me the chance I was looking for by giving me a bedroom which opened into the one occupied by my young cousin. I did not dare pay her a visit the first night. I wished to feel my way first and see how she would take my advances. She had given me a friendly embrace on my arrival, but that was not enough to encourage me to take any more serious liberties with her.

'In the morning I rose before she did; it was already broad daylight. I softly opened the door and peeped in; she was still asleep, but her breasts were entirely bare.

'I tiptoed near to see if I could catch a glimpse of her sweet grotto of love, and succeeded in seeing the whole of her fine little cunt as she just then made a movement, giving me a full exhibition of the works I was determined to penetrate before night had passed.

'I tumbled back into bed again and jerked myself off. Chance brought us together a short while before dinner and I took occasion to compliment her upon her appearance and she returned the compliment.

' "But I have not got such pretty things as you have on your breast."

' "There is nothing strange about that, you would have it if you were a girl."

' "Then I wish I were one. I have never seen anything nicer."

' "Hush, my aunt is coming; she will scold us. Besides, you who are ordained should not talk like this."

' "There is nothing in my vows that prevents me from admiring anything beautiful, especially for the gratification of His chosen servants, like myself, and there is nothing sinful for me to admire His creations in any form in which I may find them."

' "Oh my God! If my aunt heard you! She who has

thanked the Lord for having a saint in the family.''

'We were still talking when a servant entered. She immediately changed the subject of our conversation and a stray smile that I observed gave me an idea that I would be successful. Girls mature early, you know, Angelica, and they could give us men pointers on such matters.'

'The men have always those opinions of us and they are the very ones to start and awaken our early maturity. I suppose you found occasion to have another little private talk with her.'

'Yes, that very afternoon, about four o'clock we went together to visit some relatives of ours living a little distance out of the city. We did not stay very long and returning, took our way through the woods skirting the banks of the river.

'As a boy, I knew a hidden place and I intended to take my cousin there to continue the conversation we had had in the morning. I found the place and, saying that it was too early yet to return home, I prepared to sit down in this secluded spot and have a chat.

'She blushed and trembled but, without hesitation, she agreed. We sat down and, coming close to her, I put my arm about her waist and started to unbutton her dress, saying:

' ''Cousin dear, do you remember what we were talking about this morning? You know it is no sin to admire the work of God, so let me see your titties; instead of sinning, you will be doing a very commendable thing by allowing one of His servants to admire the beauties given you by Him.''

' ''Oh, cousin dear, do not deceive me, it is surely not wrong to expose myself thus?''

' ''Oh, you innocent, if you feel pleasure in showing me that which no one else has yet seen, it must be a good work, you are performing, for otherwise God would prevent you from feeling pleasure.''

' ''Yes, I think you are right. It gives me pleasure, especially when you are handling them as you are doing now. I have a feeling creeping over me, the like of which I have never felt before.''

' ''Do you like that feeling?'' I asked her, while I pressed hot kisses on her titties and, taking the nipples between my lips, I began to tickle them with the tip of my tongue.

'I produced the effect I intended. Her hand stole down and pressed the point above the junction of her thighs.

' ''Cousin dear,'' said I, ''if you feel pleasure where your hand is now, I must see that place too. You will do me a great favour and by doing me this favour, you will be doing something very laudable.'' With this, I put my hand beneath her skirts and began to feel for her little cunt, which was quivering with excitement under my lewd touches. She let me do as I liked and, pushing up her skirts, I feasted my eyes on her treasures.

'My hands wandered all over her mound, which was just beginning to show a little fine fleece. I pushed my finger between the half-open lips but soon her hymen hindered me and, to make her still more willing, I knelt down in front of her and began to kiss and suck her clitoris; her naturally lascivious temper now began to assert itself. Her arse began to move under my proceedings and signs of pleasure escaped her; she was ready to receive the final lesson in venery. Getting up, I released my now impatient prick, which longed to make the acquaintance of the fine little temple of love, which I continued to finger.

' ''Look here, cousin, you may as well admire my hidden beauties and caress them too, if you wish.'' With this, I felt her little hand already feeling my delighted prick; I showed her how to pull the skin back and expose the purple head, which evidently pleased her very much.

' ''What do you call this?'' she asked.

' ''This is my prick and what I am feeling is called a cunt; and these two parts are made for each other and there is no greater pleasure in this world for man and woman than putting the prick into the cunt. This action is called fucking, and if you will let me, I will fuck you for our mutual pleasure.''

' ''But, cousin, is that not sinful? But no, it cannot be, for I know that it would give me pleasure to feel this beautiful thing in here.''

' ''Now it is no sin if you do it with me, at least, but if it should be I can absolve you, but as you have remarked, it can be no sin as those parts have been made for that purpose, only we must keep this a secret between us, as there are always people who are envious of being not able to obtain any heavenly enjoyments and twist things in such a manner as to make it appear that the most innocent pleasures are sins.''

' ''That is all right, cousin. As long as you and I know we are doing nothing wrong, it is nobody else's business, and as I am sure that you only want to teach me laudable and commendable things, you may instruct me how to fuck. I am longing for that enlightment; just tell me what to do and I am sure that I will prove an apt scholar.''

' ''No doubt, my dear. I will instruct you in this right off, but before proceeding I must tell you that you will experience at first intense pain, until your little cunt has been stretched sufficiently to accommodate my prick but this will be immediately followed by the most exquisite pleasures, so if you are willing to bear those pains, say so, and I will offer my prick to celebrate the first fuck in your narrow slit.''

' ''Well, I am ready, so do not lose any more time, but fuck me.''

' ''Lay back . . . take off your drawers . . . good . . . now spread your legs as much as you can.'' I then topped her, put my prick to the exceedingly small opening and began a steady pressure; after quite a while I succeeded in lodging the head between the lips. My sweetheart cried out with the pain, but this, instead of making me more tender, only increased my passion and keeping up a steady pressure I was buried in her halfway. Then, pulling back again, I asked her to buck up against me. She did so, and putting my whole force to it, I pushed at the same time, and while she cried aloud I felt my prick breaking down all obstacles and sinking into her up to the roots.

'The long-sustained excitement caused me to spend now and my spunk ran in a stream from me, oiling her splendidly and soothing the torn and lacerated parts of my young relative.

'My prick never lost any of its stiffness and I remained lodged in the sweet cunt, motionless until my little girl came to again, when she pressed me with all her might, saying:

' ''You have hurt me fearfully, but it now begins to feel good.''

' ''Well, shall I begin to move again?''

' ''Yes, but slowly at first . . . that is nice. Now a little faster . . . tell me what to do, shall I move up as before . . . yes, that is nice . . . faster now . . . faster . . . Oh! this is the best ever. I thank you for having taught me this. Ah, I must cross my legs over your back, oh, now it is going in deeper. Ah, I feel something flowing from me . . . do not . . . pull out . . . leave it . . . where it is.''

'She had spent for the first time, but her desires were not satisfied yet for she treated my prick to a series of pressures, making me feel that I did not want to leave this enchanted place, so I took another turn out of her, then we got up and hurried home. On the way thither I told her that I intended to sleep with her the coming night and she was delighted with it.

'So when I retired I went directly to her room and found my cousin already in bed, waiting for me, and during that night and all the following ones of my stay, I gave her instructions in the art of fucking and she certainly proved an apt scholar. She was, and is today, one of the hottest pieces of cunt that I ever met, excepting you, my dear Angelica, and this is the story of the loss of my maidenhead.'

'What became of your cousin?'

'She is today my sister-in-law and, as I return every year for a few weeks at the old home, we repeat the lessons, and if I had to embrace the priesthood to please my mother for the purpose of leaving most of the estate to my older brother, I have taken the task upon myself to make the children for him and, as I am a good deal better furnished than he is, my sister-in-law is delighted to help me all she can. Out of four that she bore him, I can with right claim to be the father of three of them, among whom was the first born.

'I fucked her the night before the wedding continously from ten in the evening till six in the morning. She tried to outdo me and succeeded in stiffening my prick nine times before I could cry for quarter.

'Before the ceremony I had to hear her confession in the sacristy and instead of doing this, I fingered her cunt and she my prick, till she had me stiff again, then kneeling down on the floor, she made me fuck her dog fashion twice; oh, she is certainly a hot piece, for she asked me to get the chaplain to look after her in my absence, and he, being a friend of mine, is helping her out with his prick.'

This story had made my cousin so hot that she asked Dom Delabrise if he could not quench the fire he had kindled. I took pity on Felicity, made her kneel where she was, uncovered her from behind and made Delabrise mount and give her a good poking.

The time had now come for Delabrise to leave and, after taking me in his arms, he expressed the hope of meeting me well the next time. Then he left.

A few days after this I received word that I would be permitted to take the black veil and that in consideration, therefore, I should employ the intervening time in visiting my people. In consequence, my mother called at the convent to take me home.

My companions exacted a promise from me that I would write frequently and let them know how I was getting along. How I kept my promise may be seen from the following letters:

My dear Felicity:

I arrived Thursday at my parents' home; no one could have had a grander reception. One glance told me that many changes had taken place since I had left. I understand that the Bishop of — is responsible for most of these changes and that he has furnished the funds to fit out the house in its present luxurious style.

I have not had the pleasure of making his acquaintance but we expect him in a few days and then I shall be able to tell you what he looks like. My sister treats me with genuine sisterly affection.

One afternoon, while we were together doing some work, she told me the life in the convent was the best that a woman could adopt and she said that she would one day most likely follow my example.

Now, knowing that her cunt had earned all the wealth surrounding me, I had a time to suppress my mirth at this hypocritical talk. I pretend to be very innocent and I had to bite my lips more than once to keep from bursting out laughing.

I expect to keep on playing the guileless innocent until I have succeeded in getting behind the secret of this little whore, my sister, and the Bishop.

I am desirous of seeing you and my lover again. Remember me to him and to the ladies whom we consider our intimate friends.

I am your loving cousin,

ANGELICA

'Dear Felicity:

I cried with joy on on reading your letter, I have had the pleasure of meeting the Bishop and of dining with him. He is a handsome man and was politeness personified. He even offered me his services should I have need of them. I do not doubt but he would be willing to contribute to an increase in my income.

He has for a servant a young lackey, quite good looking, who, if I am not mistaken, takes more than an ordinary interest in my sister's maid, to which she is not at all indifferent. His Excellency acted with the utmost reserve towards his lady love while I was present, but in spite of all their precautions I noticed that their eyes, whenever they met, talked most eloquently the language of love and I believe that they repaid themselves for their compulsory restraint the very next night, for they slept together.

This is all the information I can give you this time, but I have devised a plan whereby I can spy on them without being seen and, in my next letter, I may be able to give some interesting news.

I have not yet made the acquaintance of the Bishop's nephew, but if he tries to make love to me, he will receive a cold reception, for if he is as handsome as Adonis, I will not love him.

Preserve your strength, so that when I return, I may show you that I am as ever,

Your most affectionate cousin

ANGELICA

Dear Angelica:

I enclose a letter from Dom Delabrise. He begged me to explain to you how it came about that this letter was so long delayed, and I assured him that you would not be angry with him. We talked about you a great deal and, knowing that you would be thankful for anything that would console him, I took your place and had him fuck me four times, so that he could enjoy your embrace by proxy, so to speak. Adieu, darling.

Yours,

FELICITY

Dear Felicity:

I am delighted to hear that you saw fit to console my poor Delabrise with your own charms and, when you see him again, tell him that I am longing to be with him again.

I have finally caught our lovers at some of their

amatory combats and will tell you how I managed it.

Having examined the garret directly over my sister's room, I employed the better part of three days that my sister was away from home to make an opening in the floor of the garret so that I could get a good view of her room, taking care to make it so that nothing could be seen in the ceiling.

On the same day that my sister returned home, the Bishop called to see her. That was about four o'clock in the afternoon. After supper I took leave of the company, saying that I wished to retire. So I went to bed early and was up again at five in the morning, ready for all emergencies.

I dressed myself immediately and stole softly to the garret, leaving my shoes at the door which I closed after me. On tiptoe, I slipped over to the hole in the floor and put my eye to it, stretching myself at full length on the floor; this gave me an easy and comfortable position and I could observe all that took place in the room below, which I believed was the temple where my sister sacrificed to Venus.

It was already broad daylight and the blinds and curtains were thrown back. The lovers, still asleep, were partly uncovered. My mouth watered at the sight of the long big prick lying so nicely between the Bishop's thighs. I had held my post nearly an hour before they began to stir and finally they woke up.

The first move my sister made was to put her hand on the still-limber prick. She evidently was experienced in handling his dart. She began shoving the skin back and forth, uncovering the head and then pulling the skin over it again, while with the other hand she played with the bag underneath. Then she took the prick between her two hands, rolling it between her palms. Seeing that her work was about to be crowned with success, she got up and knelt well over the Bishop in such a manner that her cunt was just above his face and her face above his prick. No sooner was she in this position than the Bishop began to kiss her cunt and suck it, while she reciprocated in the same manner on his prick; no sooner had she succeeded in getting it entirely stiff than she jumped up and, bringing her gaping bijou over his prick, she let herself slowly down upon it, burying it to the root in her happy cunt.

I could see that she was well educated in all the refined ways of making love, for she rode her lover with consummate skill. He must have been on the verge of spending when I heard him mutter the word 'arsehole', and my sister understanding his wishes, allowed the stately prick to slip out of her cunt and, taking hold of it, she lodged it in the neighboring hole and made it disappear between her big cheeks. The Bishop grunted with satisfaction and, reaching under the pillow, he handed a big dildo to my sister. She quickly inserted it in her cunt and kept working it there, while she at the same time flew up and down on the Bishop's prick, who shouted:

'Ah, my dear, you kill me with pleasure! You are the best little whore I ever had the luck to possess. You never leave anything to wish for; you always know how to please my most lascivious ideas; I do not think that there is anything for you to learn in the way of whoring!'

'Oh yes, I think there is, but I have learned all

that I know from you; you have been fingering my cunt since I was barely sixteen years old and at that time you made me suck your prick and a year later you buggered me; and when I succeed in giving you satisfaction now, it is because you taught me and I know what your wishes are and try to anticipate them because I am grateful for all that you have taught me and because I love you for that.

'But I really think there is yet more to learn in the way of lechery and I know where I could learn some new ideas, that is, in the fine brothels of Paris, and understand me well, for your sake, I would stay in one of them for a few weeks only, to be still better able to satisfy your licentious cravings.

'You are a jewel to propose what I had not dared to propose to you, fearing you might be offended, but now as you have proposed it, you will do as you said. I will foot the bill and to show my gratitude I will buy a country estate for you and settle enough on you to make you independent, should I die suddenly; but enough of that now; I am coming – do you feel it squirting into you, pet?'

'Yes, your hot spunk fills my whole entrails, but finish me off, please, work the dildo for me. That is right! Shove it up as far as it goes . . . ah I am spending!'

She got up now and went to the bidet to cleanse herself, then, returning to the bed, she performed the same operation on the prick of her lover.

I had seen enough and heard enough, so I left my place of concealment, went to my room and had to take my finger to quiet my lewd feelings caused by the spectacle which I had witnessed. In the afternoon the Bishop's nephew called. I had very little conversation with him. I could see by the way he eyed me that I would suit his lustful purpose very well, but he displeased me and I will give him such a send-off the first time that he speaks of love that he will lose all hope of ever possessing me then and there.

Please hand the enclosed letter to Dom Delabrise, it may bring him out of the deep gloom. Let me hear from you often and rest assured that I am,

Your affectionate cousin,

ANGELICA

Dear Felicity,

I am glad to know that I will find a new companion when I return to you. I have been treated to another view of two lovers, but before I begin to tell you what I saw, I must tell you about myself and how I was treated by my cousin and the Bishop's nephew.

Sunday afternoon I was sitting in my room, writing to Dom Delabrise, when my cousin entered and signified a desire to speak to me privately. I hastily covered the letter I was writing and invited him to take a seat near me.

He was quite agitated, his face was paler than usual and I thought I could detect the odor of liquor on his breath. He began by telling me his troubles and his ambitions, how he would like to be a lieutenant in the army and that the Bishop's nephew was the one to procure the appointment for him, and how he was deeply in debt and that the Bishop's nephew held nearly all his notes and that he would surely be ruined if the aforesaid nephew was not appeased.

I listened till he had finished and then I told him how I felt about the matter. My life was devoted to the Church and God, I would do all I possibly could for him, even go to the Bishop in his behalf, but as for the nephew, he was out of the question.

I tried in every way to calm him, but all my efforts had directly the opposite effect. He was becoming more and more excited; he pleaded and threatened in turn. I was becoming alarmed and made a move to leave the room. My crazy cousin got between me and the door and would not let me pass.

'No, you can't leave here,' he said between his teeth, 'till you listen to reason; my future depends on it.'

The Bishop's nephew then came in and added his entreaties to those of my cousin. I was now thoroughly aroused. I flew at him like a tigress and commanded them to let me pass. I rushed at my cousin and tried to push him aside. He grabbed me roughly around the waist and held me. I attempted to scream, but he placed his hand over my mouth and would not let me.

He made some motion with his head to the Bishop's nephew and, as if prearranged, the latter bolted and shut the door from the inside and then drew the blinds.

I was struggling all the time to free myself and in the scuffle was thrown to the floor. The Bishop's nephew now knelt down and tried to turn my head so that he could kiss me. I scratched his hands and spat in his face, but in spite of all that I could do, he managed to put his mouth to mine. Then he began to fumble under my skirts.

I did my best to kick him, but he caught me by the ankles and raised my legs up so that my petticoats fell down off them and my whole lower parts were exposed to the lascivious glances of the cur. I could struggle no longer. I was completely exhausted. My cousin saw that and let go of my head.

The nephew then threw himself full length upon me and forced my legs with his knees. By wriggling my hips first one way, then another, I kept him from getting his prick into me for some time, but at last I felt it slip in.

The excitement of the struggle had nearly done the work for him, for he had not given half a dozen passionate shoves before he finished. I could feel that he had a much larger and thicker prick than my cunt had ever felt before and I was beginning to feel good when he stopped. He then rolled off and held me while my cousin took his place.

After a few moments the pleasure became too much for me, I could not contain myself any longer. I threw my legs over my cousin's back in the heat of passion and glued my lips to his, while I shoved my arse to meet him halfway, to heighten the pleasure. The Bishop's nephew was frigging my areshole and my fully aroused clitoris.

I have found pleasure with Dom Delabrise, I have found pleasure with the Franciscan and with one of my own sex, but the pleasure I experienced now was never equalled before.

My cousin finished and got off me, but the Bishop's nephew was not yet satisfied, so he mounted me again. This time he treated me to slow and deliberate shoves. At first I made some pretence of repelling him, but his shaft had not worked out and in a dozen times when I surrendered unconditionally and when he asked me if I would like a change of positions, I was more than willing.

He got up, made my cousin lie down on his back. I had to kneel over my cousin, one knee each side of his head, then the Bishop's nephew mounted me from behind, driving his stallion's prick into me with one mighty shove. I felt it touch way up at the entrance of my womb. At the same time I felt my cousin's tongue tickling my clitoris and with one finger he was buried in my arsehole. It was more pleasure than I had ever had before.

I bent over and took the now stiff prick of my cousin into my mouth and paid back his efforts on my behalf. Before long the sexual spasm overcame me and the Bishop's nephew, but he was a prudent man so, pulling out, he forced the next entrance and there deposited his burning spunk.

We now repeated this performance, only the men changed places. Both now had all they wanted for a little while at least, so they assisted me to rise and allowed me to sit on a chair.

They both asked my forgiveness for what they had done to me and, as I was not hurt, it was easy to forgive, after the intense delight they had given me. They next brought out some wine and plied me with it and I soon became half-drunk.

I got frolicsome, talked and laughed; they exchanged lewd glances and I didn't resist in the least when they began to put me into a complete state of nakedness.

I was getting drunk and I only dimly remember that the two men, one in the front and the other behind, violated me from both sides at the same time. I know I felt a sharp pain in my rectum and I heard a voice give an exclamation of satisfaction and that is all I remember till I awoke some three hours later, none the worse for my experience.

My cousin got his commission in the army and his debts were paid. To compensate myself in a measure, I made my cousin sleep with me for the few nights he is to stay at home and he has taught me a few tricks in the way of procuring sexual pleasure.

A few nights ago he told me that if I would consent to meet him and the Bishop's nephew in my bedroom and submit to their assaults, the Bishop's nephew would settle two thousand livres a year on me and as I have noticed that the political situation is such a one that it is quite possible that all the convents will be suppressed, I have consented as much for you and Dom Delabrise as my own sake, for that will give us the means to stay together even if such calamities should happen to religious orders.

Last night, being alone at home with my cousin, the Bishop's nephew took me to my sister's room, where they both seemed to be well acquainted; for they got out of the hidden drawers all sorts of contrivances to be used to commit various kinds of sexual excesses; dildos of all kinds and sizes, switches, whip books and lewd scenes.

In the course of the night all these things came into use and I must say that what those two devils do not know about increasing the delights of love is not worth knowing; they used or rather misused me in every possible way, but I could not expect to get off so easy when such a price had been paid me, and, really, I was thankful for the experience. Besides, I found out that my sister deceives the Bishop and that his nephew as well as my cousin come in for a share of her favors.

To return to the Bishop, he spent a week in the country with my sister, who returned alone, saying that the Bishop would follow her in a few days. On the eve of her return I heard my sister give some rather strange instructions to her maid: to wake her at a very early hour the next morning, as she wished to be ready by eight o'clock.

I determined to be up as early as she. I hurried to take up my station at the peephole, but imagine my astonishment to see my sister already up, standing there stark-naked, the hair of her grotto of love all done up in curl papers and her maid kneeling before her comb in hand. I had to push my handkerchief into my mouth to keep from laughing right out.

My sister sat down and spread her legs apart; then the maid proceeded to take the papers out, leaving a nice little curl where the papers had been; then some dark brown powder was thrown on the curls to make the surrounding flesh look whiter and then they were trimmed so that not a single hair stood out further than its neighbor.

The maid now rubbed her body with essences, after which she threw on a light wrapper, neatly made.

A delicate pink shirt with delicate embroidery, a skirt of the same which covered only half of one leg, completed her apparel. Then my sister, thus dressed, stretched herself unconcernedly on the sofa, awaiting the arrival of the Bishop. The maid, also stark-naked, stood in a position that exposed her cunt to advantage.

The Bishop entered. He wore a long trailing robe, whose train was carried by his lackey, and looked for all the world like the Great Mogul entering the harem quarters.

He stood for a moment admiring the two Venuses, he praised the maid for the taste she showed in dressing cunts and the maid fell on her knees before him and, taking his exposed prick into her mouth, gave it a hearty suck, this being done in place of the customary kiss on the hand.

He now gave free reign to his passions. He swooped down upon my sister and attacked her with passionate vigor. As for me, I pushed a dildo into my burning cunt and soon brought down a plentiful spend.

After relieving myself I went back to my post and saw my sister being fucked in the front by the lackey and in the rear by the Bishop, while the maid was licking the latter's arsehole and working an enormous dildo in and out of her cunt. They finally finished, all four at the one time.

There, my dear cousin, is what I have been up to. Next week I will return and then we will try to imitate some of these actions with the aid of some of our gentlemen friends. In the meantime, I am,

Affectionately yours,

ANGELICA

Angelica returned to the Abbey and took the veil, but a few weeks afterwards the government confiscated the property of the convents and then Angelica, Felicity and

Suzanne and some others emigrated together with their lovers to America, where they married and founded a little colony and prospered and continued at their old games.

A selection of bestsellers from Headline

FICTION

BLOOD STOCK	John Francome & James MacGregor	£3.99 ☐
THE OLD SILENT	Martha Grimes	£4.50 ☐
ALL THAT GLITTERS	Katherine Stone	£4.50 ☐
A FAMILY MATTER	Nigel Rees	£4.50 ☐
EGYPT GREEN	Christopher Hyde	£4.50 ☐

NON-FICTION

MY MOUNTBATTEN YEARS	William Evans	£4.50 ☐
WICKED LADY Salvador Dali's Muse	Tim McGirk	£4.99 ☐
THE FOOD OF SPAIN AND PORTUGAL	Elisabeth Lambert Ortiz	£5.99 ☐

SCIENCE FICTION AND FANTASY

REVENGE OF THE FLUFFY BUNNIES Cineverse Cycle Book 3	Craig Shaw Gardner	£3.50 ☐
BROTHERS IN ARMS	Lois McMaster Bujold	£4.50 ☐
THE SEA SWORD	Adrienne Martine-Barnes	£3.50 ☐
NO HAVEN FOR THE GUILTY	Simon Green	£3.50 ☐
GREENBRIAR QUEEN	Sheila Gilluly	£4.50 ☐

All Headline books are available at your local bookshop or newsagent, or can be ordered direct from the publisher. Just tick the titles you want and fill in the form below. Prices and availability subject to change without notice.

Headline Book Publishing PLC, Cash Sales Department, PO Box 11, Falmouth, Cornwall, TR10 9EN, England.

Please enclose a cheque or postal order to the value of the cover price and allow the following for postage and packing:
UK: 80p for the first book and 20p for each additional book ordered up to a maximum charge of £2.00
BFPO: 80p for the first book and 20p for each additional book
OVERSEAS & EIRE: £1.50 for the first book, £1.00 for the second book and 30p for each subsequent book.

Name ....

Address ....

....

....